Familiar

By Brianna Demaree

Chapter 1

The bell rang for seventh period to begin at Amington High school. It was Friday; the last class of the day, fifty minutes and the captive students would be home free for the weekend. The pre-calculus classroom was already full of students, but in the back corner of the room, three senior-grade girls stood crowded around a single desk.

Sitting at the desk was a teenage boy. He was eighteen and looked like your typical punk rock emo kid, complimentary with rock t-shirts and the daily overdose of too much black. The teen had black hair that fell to around his shoulders in length, but the teen always kept his hair pulled back in a high ponytail. Only his bangs, which were too short to stay contained within the confines of the ponytail, fell and framed his face. His dark hair and pale complexion only intensified the blue of his eyes which were currently transfixed on the deck of tarot cards in his hands as he shuffled them. His name was Ash Starnes, a senior at Amington High school. "What can I do for you today? A fortune teller? A problem solver?" Ash asked the girls, still shuffling the cards.

A girl sat down in the chair across from him and laid five dollars down on the desk. The girl's name was Jessica Norton. Along with Jessica were her two friends, Amy Grace and Claire Whitstaff; the girls were frequent customers Ash's.

Jessica thought over what type of spread she wanted. "A problem solver, I think." Jessica requested just before her phone buzzed alerting her of an incoming text message.

    Ash shuffled one last time and laid out three cards face down on the desk in front of him. He set the other cards aside and pocketed the fortune fee of five dollars that Jessica previously laid on the table.

    "What's the problem?" Ash questioned, trying to get a better understanding of Jessica's situation to provide a more thorough card reading.

    "I've been talking to this guy and he just admitted that he likes me. But I'm not entirely certain about him. We've been texting for, like, two months now and I think it's starting to get serious. I want to know if he's the right guy for me." Jessica explained, looking up from her phone for a second to answer Ash before returning to text the guy back.

    "I gotcha. Let's see what the cards have to say." Ash flipped over the first card for Jessica's reading.

    Ash was a nice guy, but most people avoided him. Rumors around school said that he was into the occult and worshiped the devil, but it was nothing more than rumors. Ash did not really care what others thought of him and he was not very sociable, meaning that Ash did not have many friends. The closest thing he had to friends were a group of band kids who periodically came together to play a really popular role-playing card game called 'Spellcaster' every other weekend. Only occasionally did the kids invite Ash to come play with them. The band kids always became frustrated with Ash due to the teen being unbeatable in almost any type of card game.

The first card Ash flipped over held an image of a man and a woman standing on a body of water as they lean toward each other as if going for a kiss. The two each held a golden chalice which was connected by a semicircular beam of light glinting off the moon above them. "This card is called 'Two of Cups'," Ash explained, "It represents a deep emotional connection or attraction."

"Are you saying that we were meant to be?" Jessica smiled, finally looking at what Ash was doing as she momentarily ignored the incoming barrage of text messages her boyfriend was sending.

"I'm not saying anything, I am merely just repeating what the cards are trying to tell you. The cards say that there's a special connection of some type, but they don't specify what." Ash flipped over the second card.

The next card showed an image of a red devil complete with horns, a tail, and wings standing before a pentagram with flames surrounding him.

"The name of this card is 'The Devil'." Ash sighed and rubbed his chin. "Typically this isn't a very good card to get," Ash informed Jessica.

"Why not? I thought the worse card you can get was the death card." Jessica said, confused.

"No," Ash chuckled at the misinterpretation. "That's a stereotype that everyone gets wrong. The 'Death' card is actually one of the best cards in the deck. But anyway, this card means that there's going to be a choice, situation, or an action you'll commit which will be contrary to your best interests." Ash explained. "This may be something as simple as you and this guy getting into a fight or something."

Ash flipped over the last card; it showed a beautiful blindfolded woman clothed in white robes. She carried a scale with a sun's insignia on the pivot fulcrum and stood between two pillars as the crescent moon shined behind her. "The final card is called 'Justice'. This card represents the consequences of your actions. I know that sounds intimidating, but it's not. This card doesn't necessarily make this a bad spread. But it does mean one thing, and that is that there will be some type of offender in the situation. Whether you are the offender, it's your boyfriend, or it's someone else; they will have to face the consequences of their actions." Ash looked over the cards ready to give his final run through analysis.

The final run through was an attempt for Ash to help his customers better understand the possible results of the reading.

"You have an emotional connection to this guy that you're seeing. Unfortunately, one of you is going to commit an action or make a choice that isn't in your best interests. The closest thing I can think of as an example is maybe someone cheating on the other and getting caught. Whatever happens, the perpetrator is going to have to face the consequences of their actions at the hands of whoever was victimized."

Jessica nodded; staying silent for a spell as she thought.

"Do I need to perform a future reading?" Ash asked, ready to collect the cards.

"No, thank you. I have a decent idea with what's going on." Jessica smiled and stood with her friends. "Thanks, the cards really helped."

Ash gave a wave and collected his cards to shuffle again. He took a quick glance at the clock in the front of the room, five more minutes until class officially began. Ash leaned back in his chair as he shuffled his deck of cards, bored. He glanced to his left where a girl by the name Trisha Roxwell sat in her assigned seat.

Trisha had long, wavy brown hair that nearly came down to her waist and flawless pale skin with a few sun-kissed freckles sprinkled across her nose. The green blouse she was currently wearing vividly pronounced the green in her hazel eyes. As she was beautiful, she was intelligent. She was an honor student and part of the gifted courses at Amington High. Even though she was on the Amington High girls' volleyball team, Trisha was not one for socializing and expressed her spirit through drawings. Rumor had it, that she was pretty skilled with a pencil and a sketch pad. Trisha was shy, though, and only really talked to one person, her best friend.

Ash looked over at her as she doodled on a sketch pad. "Whatcha working on?"

Trisha looked up, startled that someone was actually talking to her and hugged her drawing to her chest so Ash could not see.

Ash grinned. "Sorry, didn't mean to startle you."

"It's okay." Trisha pushed a piece of her bangs behind her ear.

Ash watched her as she looked back down at her notebook, trying to return to the state before Ash started talking to her. "Have you ever had your fortune told before?"

Trisha curiously looked back up at Ash. "No..."

With his foot, Ash pushed the seat across from him out and patted the table. "Let me give you a reading, free of charge."

"Are you sure?" Trisha asked, nervously.

"Absolutely. Come. Sit." Ash insisted and shuffled his deck of cards.

Trisha walked over and sat in the seat across from Ash. "Is this okay?" She asked, timidly.

"Yeah. Perfect." Ash smiled, assuring her. He finished shuffling the deck and looked up at her. "Have you ever had a tarot card reading before?"

Trisha shook her head, 'no'.

"Well, since this is your first time. I'll perform a fortune reading. But if you had a problem I can do problem solvers and other services as well." Ash laid out three cards and paused when he saw Nicholas Russell walk into class.

Nicholas, or Nic, was Trisha's best friend; the only one that Trisha really talked to. Due to the two being inseparable since first grade, most in Amington High just assumed that the two were a couple even though they were just friends.

Nic walked over to his desk, which was right in front of Ash's, and set his backpack down.

Like Trisha, Nic was an honor student in the gifted courses. He was the top of the class, in the lead to be valedictorian in the spring if he kept his grades up. Ash highly doubted that would be a problem for Nic. Nic was very studious and responsible about things such as grades.

Ash had known Nic for a long time, they use to be the best of friends in kindergarten and first grade, but that was before Trisha moved to Amington and the two split up. Ash and Nic had not really talked since.

Nic had short golden blonde hair that was just a little messy yet just long enough for someone to run one's fingers through it. Nic's emerald green eyes were constantly hidden behind a pair of reading glasses, which he only wore during school hours. Nic currently wore a gray t-shirt with a plaid red and blue over shirt with the sleeves rolled up to his elbows. Unlike Trisha, Nic was not on any sports teams. Instead, Nic focused his attention primarily on music. Recently, he had been practicing a lot for a recital on violin. Amington University was offering a full ride scholarship and Nic qualified. All Nic had to do was play for a panel of College Board executives and he would be a shoe-in. Asides from violin, Nic could play almost anything ranging from drums, piano, guitar, saxophone, and so on. Nic was a prodigy, as most teachers would say.

Nic strolled over and stood by Trisha, investigating for himself what was going on.

Trisha looked up at Nic and smiled, "Hi."

"Hey, what's up?" Nic asked, leaning against the side of his desk, right beside Trisha.

"Ash was going to read my future." Trisha smiled and looked down at her hands slightly embarrassed.

"I thought you didn't believe in this type of stuff."

"I don't really, but Ash offered and I thought it would be kind of fun to see what I get." Trisha justified herself to Nic.

Ash glanced from Trisha to Nic. "Do you want me to begin?"

"Yes please." Trisha requested with a small smile.

Ash flipped over the first card which showed a tall brick tower being hit by lightning. The top of the tower was breaking off as the rest of the tower burned. The card depicted a man who jumped out of the burning tower and was falling to the ground below. "The first card represents the past," Ash explained. "This card is called 'The Tower'. It says that there was an unexpected event in your life that changed some things. Did you have anything like that happen to you?"

Trisha looked at the card. "No, the only adventurous thing that has happened to me recently was my car breaking down yesterday. I sat on the side of the road for an hour until my dad came and picked me up. It was kind of embarrassing." She laughed nervously at herself and the memory of sitting on the side of the road waiting for her father in the traffic.

Ash nodded "It could be something as simple as a car breaking down, let's see what your present is." Ash flipped over the next card which pictured a man grieving while five cups laid on the ground around him. Two cups were bright and golden, they stood erect behind the grieving man as the other three cups laid before the man, dull and broken. "This card is the 'Five of Cups'. It means that you will experience loss and grief." Ash explained.

"Yeah, I probably will when I see the repair bill for my car." Trisha giggled, feeling a little more comfortable with Ash. "Wow, this is pretty cool. I never had my fortune told."

Nic watched, silent as Trisha awed at the cards.

Ash flipped over the final card which represented the future. It showed a woman sitting on a throne between two pillars with a crescent moon shining brightly behind her. The woman wore beautiful white robes with a blue sash across her chest and held a scroll in her lap with water at her feet.

"She's pretty," Trisha commented quietly, observing the new card.

"This is 'The High Priestess'," Ash informed Trisha.

"What does she mean?" Trisha asked.

Ash cast his glance to the side and viewed Nic observing the tarot card reading, almost like he was interested.

"The 'High Priestess' represents something that can only be understood through experience," Ash explained to both of them.

Nic chuckled. "Like observing the check engine light from now on," He teased Trisha.

Trisha pursed her lips and mildly punched Nic in the arm, making him laugh harder. "Shut up. My car's getting fixed, Meanie."

Ash let Trisha look at her cards one more time before he collected them and began to shuffle.

"That was really interesting Ash, thank you." Trisha smiled and stood.

"Anytime," Ash smiled in return as he shuffled his card deck.

Trisha looked up at Nic, who stood at her side. "You should get a fortune reading."

Nic laughed and shook his head. "I'm good, Trish."

"Please?" Trisha gently tugged on the sleeve of his shirt.

Nic sighed and pulled out the chair Trisha vacated only a few moments before, sitting down across from Ash.

Nic pulled out his wallet from his pocket and laid a ten dollar bill on the desk. "That's for Trisha's fortune as well as mine."

"Thanks, but it was free," Ash said.

"Just take the money."

Ash shrugged and pocketed the money.

"I really don't want to do this." Nic sighed and watched Ash shuffle the cards.

"Scared?" Ash smirked, he got that answer sometimes. Since Ash's predictions were so accurate, most thought he was talking to the devil through the cards or some such nonsense. But again, that was just another stupid high school rumor.

"I'm hardly scared of some $.99 playing cards." Nic muttered a bit bored and rested his elbow on the desk to support his head.

Ash gave Nic an irritated look which Nic did not see. Ash shuffled and drew three cards which he laid face down on his desk.

Preferably Ash would rather not tell Nic's fortune, but it was a job and he was not willing to pass up easy money. He took a breath and flipped over the first card.

The card had a picture of a jester carrying a knapsack looking up at the sky as a dog followed him at his heels. The sun is shining in the background and before the jester is a cliff which he appears oblivious to.

"Fool," Ash muttered.

Nic heard him and snapped out of his daze to look at Ash, "Excuse me?"

"Your card is 'The Fool'." Ash clarified. "It represents the coming to a crossroad in life that you are unaware of," Ash explained, "Since 'The Fool' is the first card I flipped, he is the past card, meaning that you have already come to that crossroad and were unaware of it."

Nic was confused.

Ash flipped over the middle card, just wanting to get Nic's reading over with. If it was any other person, he would slow down and talk about each card in more detail to explain it to them so they could get a better understand of the meaning of their cards. But currently, Ash did not want to talk to Nic. Maybe it was because Ash was jealous, but the teen was not entirely certain.

The middle card showed a skeleton horseman carrying a flag of a white rose with mortal humans bowed before the rider. "This card is 'Death'," Ash said, showing the card to Nic.

Nic looked at the card, a little bored. "Isn't this a little dramatic?" He asked, examining the card of the skeleton.

"The card of 'Death' rarely means physical death. The 'Death' card focuses primarily on transformations and new beginnings. The 'Death' represents an ending that makes transformations possible and brings about new things." Ash enlightened and turned over Nic's final card, the future card. The final card showed a blindfolded woman holding two swords and sitting on a stool-like bench with the sea behind her and a crescent moon in the sky overhead.

Nic looked at the final card. Ash had piqued his interest with the 'Death' card. "What does that mean?" Nic asked.

"Your future card is the 'Two of Swords'. This card represents a conflict of mind and heart. Your fortune is very interesting, I would say-,"Ash was cut off before he could properly give an interpretation as Mrs. Sandra, the pre-calculus teacher, walked into class as the bell rang for seventh period to officially begin.

"Everyone in their seats." Mrs. Sandra instructed, holding a stack of pop quizzes. "It's Friday! Everyone knows what that means!" She basically sang.

A chorus of 'awes' erupted in the room.

"I know. I'm such a horrible person. I can't imagine a teacher who makes their students learn things." She satirically said, not sympathizing with her students one bit as she handed out the quizzes by walking down the aisles.

Ash watched Nic as he sat in his assigned seat in front of him.

For some reason, Ash had this horrible feeling but pushed any thought of it aside as Mrs. Sandra placed a quiz on his desk. Ash picked up his pencil and looked at the empty graphs and complex formulas. Ash then prayed that he would get credit if he, at least, put his name on the top of the quiz.

Chapter 2

    Ash hated pre-calculus with a burning passion. He did not understand it and it was one of those classes that he knew he would never use the information he was learning ever again in the future.

    Ash was not exactly the perfect student, he was borderline failing most of his classes. His view was as long as he could graduate, he really did not care how bad his grades got. For now, Ash pushed every thought about grades and classes out of his mind. It was the weekend, he could finally go home to relax and not worry about pop quizzes or other such school-related nonsense.

    Ash walked out through the front doors with the other students as they walked home, to their cars, or to the buses.

    Ash lived not far from the school, but it was a bit of a walk. He had his own car, but he did not favor driving. Ash would take the bus, but it was always too cramped and noisy. So, Ash walked; he enjoyed walking and taking in the cool November air. Fall was here and it was very evident on the trees as their leaves were beginning to turn from lively green to lifeless orange and brown. The teen dug in his backpack and pulled out a cheap sci-fi novel which he opened to a bookmarked page and began to read as he walked home.

    Ash lived in the suburbs like everyone, but along his street the houses were much bigger, closely resembling small mansions.

At 666 Livian street, an 1800's Victorian styled mansion stood amongst the other multi-story modern houses lined down the street. Everyone in Amington called it the 'Haunted Mansion', it looked run down and decrepit. Anyone passing by would say that it was abandoned, but rumors constantly buzzed around campus and the town that the house was either haunted or owned by witches. Ash did not know which rumor started first, but they were a jumbled mess nowadays.

The house was the home of a popular psychic in Amington, Ash's Uncle Jacob. Just like Ash, Uncle Jacob was unique and had special abilities normal people would consider supernatural. Uncle Jacob opened a psychic business in his own home and people sought him out, seeking their fortunes told and knowing that his predictions held spot-on accuracy.

Ash lived with Uncle Jacob, who was not related to him by blood or marriage. It was a long confusing story that Ash did not want to delve into. But basically, he had been living with Uncle Jacob since he was born.

Ash walked up the pathway to the manor-like house and climbed the front steps of the porch. He opened the front door and entered his home. Beyond the front door was the living room. It was of simple design; three black leather couches surrounded a fireplace. To the right of the fireplace was a door which leads to the store room where Jacob performed his psychic readings for paying customers and to the left of the fireplace was another door which leads down to the basement. The living room was white with black trimmings and the walls sported a few monochrome abstract pieces of art. A black grand piano stood beside the grand stairwell to add some personality to the room. No one in Ash's family could play an instrument, so anything musical within the household was purely for aesthetics. Shielded by the stairwell was a hallway which led to the kitchen, dining room, and laundry room.

Ash closed the front door behind him and watched a woman cleaning the fireplace. The woman wore a formal maid outfit consisting of a white dress shirt, gray vest, and a black miniskirt that was currently coming up in the back. As she bent over the fireplace, she gave Ash a flash of pink checkered panties.

Ash hid his blushing face behind his book. "Shima, your skirt. Please fix yourself," He politely ordered.

The woman, Shima, sighed and stood up to straighten herself. Shima appeared to be in her mid-twenties and had long black hair which fell past her waist. When Shima turned around, Ash could finally see that her white dress shirt was soiled with ash and other debris from the filthy fireplace. Shima's gray vest acted more like a corset which pushed up her breasts and she consistently wears her dress shirt unbuttoned very low to reveal serious cleavage. Shima's attire constantly made Ash worry that Shima would be spilling out at any second. Dangling between her breasts was a simple low hanging necklace, consisting of a baby blue ribbon and a silver bell. Shima situated her skirt, smoothing it down for Ash.

She looked up and met Ash's blue eyes with vibrant blood red eyes before bowing. "Welcome back Ash."

"Where's Uncle Jacob?" Ash asked, walking over to the stairs and hanging onto the banister of the grand staircase.

"Master Jacob is in his study," Shima informed Ash, watching as the teen threw his backpack onto the closest couch.

"Thanks and can you take that up to my room?" Ash's request was more of an order as he walked up the stairs and down the hall to his Uncle's study, abandoning the backpack.

Shima returned to her previous task of cleaning the fireplace.

The inside of the house was definitely different from the outside, it was like being inside a real manor. The sophisticated décor, the stately cleanliness, and the top notch service was all Shima's doing. Ash walked down the hallway and stopped at a specific door and knocked. No one answered, so he continued inside to find his Uncle passed out at his desk with a bottle of wine in his hand.

Ash sighed and walked over to his Uncle. Ash gently shook his Uncle's shoulder in an attempt to wake him up. "Uncle Jacob?"

Jacob snorted and it woke him from his nap. "Huh?" He asked, rubbing his head. He picked up his glasses and put them on, looking up at Ash with sleepy green eyes.

Ash's Uncle appeared about thirty and wore his waist length sandy blond hair in a ponytail. He was a formal dresser always wearing trousers with a dress shirt and a vest. His uncle stood and picked up a leather bound book he was just previously using as a pillow and walked over to a bookshelf. "What are you doing here? Why aren't you at school?"

"School ended thirty minutes ago," Ash informed his guardian.

"Oh…" Jacob said and scratched his head as he looked at his bookshelf.

"Guess what tonight is." Ash smiled, looking at the books on the shelf with his Uncle and pulling one out on palm reading.

"I don't even get a hint?" Jacob teased.

"It's kind of my birthday." Ash reminded him, hoping his Uncle had not forgotten.

"Ah shoot! I forgot." Jacob sighed.

Ash's eyes widened in panic. "What?!"

Jacob's serious expression broke into a fit of laughter. "You should've seen your face, Ash. Priceless." Jacob laughed and sat at his desk. "I remembered. Shima has been cooking the brew for the spell all day in the potion room." Jacob finished laughing and wolf whistled to summon his servant, Shima.

"Yes, Master?" Shima asked, suddenly appearing beside Ash which made the teen jump back.

"How is the brew?" Jacob queried Shima.

"It's coming along nicely, my lord." She purred and sat on his desk.

"Define well," Jacob ordered.

Shima's eyes shifted, the white of her eyes turned black as her irises remained red and she smiled seductively. "It is a dark teal blue color. As it bubbles it gives off the odor of cooking meat."

"Good. It's coming along nicely; it should be attracting plenty of spirits." Jacob said, thinking aloud.

Shima's eyes returned back to their normal blood red color. "What do you request of me, Master?" Shima purred and situated the glasses on her master's face.

Ash looked away, a little embarrassed to see all of that. "Still in the room," He muttered under his breath to remind the two.

"I want you to make sure that the potion room is fully prepped for tonight." Jacob requested.

"Yes Master, consider it done." She jumped off his desk and curtsied.

"What of dinner?" Jacob asked before the beautiful woman left.

"It's ready to be served," Shima informed with a curt smile.

"You have done beautifully, my dear, thank you so much. You are dismissed." Jacob smiled and Shima left to perform her new chores.

Ash was a wizard, he was born with magical powers just like Uncle Jacob. Ash's ability with cards was strongly influenced by his magic and the type of magic he used. No one knew besides his Uncle, Shima, and the rest of the magical world. It was a well-kept secret and it was going to stay that way. Today was Ash's birthday, it was a big deal for a witch or wizard to turn eighteen. The eighteenth birthday of a witch or wizard meant that they were finally considered mature, meaning that they could care for a life of their own and create a familiar.

Familiars served their master either witch or wizard without hesitation, they are the perfect complement of their master's soul. On a witch or wizard's birthday, they make a body and see if a compatible soul attaches to the body, if it does, a familiar is formed. A typical familiar all bear the same markings, black hair and blood red eyes. A perfect example of a familiar was Jacob's familiar, Shima.

Jacob wrapped an arm around Ash's shoulders. "Come birthday boy, let's go eat." Jacob suggested and led Ash out of the study.

#####

Ash looked at the grandfather clock in the living room as the minute hand ticked closer to midnight. He sat on the couch reading a manga with his hair tied up in a bun. The bun even managed to pull up a majority of his bangs, but a few uncooperative pieces continued to fall in his eyes. Ash wore a black robe over his clothes to not mess anything up, making a familiar was messy work from what his uncle told him and it was customary that witches or wizards wore such robes over their normal clothing as a timeless tradition.

Jacob walked out from the door to the left of the fireplace dressed in a black robe as well, "Are you ready to begin?"

"I'm ready," Ash said, setting his book down and standing. He was a tad bit nervous, but he knew it was nothing to be nervous about.

"Take your time and relax." Jacob smiled, seeing how tense Ash was.

"I am relaxed." Ash said with dignity and holding his head high, still shaking.

Jacob laughed. "Uh-huh. You're doing great." Jacob led the way down a flight of stairs to the basement where Shima was stirring a boiling cauldron.

"Master, should I let it settle now?" Shima asked as she stirred the brew.

"Yes, we need to let the body form." Jacob took over, letting Shima back up.

Shima stepped back and bowed, backing all the way to the wall.

The basement was used for potion making, thus, they called it the potion room. The walls were lined with cabinets filled with potion ingredients, robes, and empty vials and bottles. A grandfather clock stood by the entrance of the basement, but in the middle of the room was a huge black cauldron filled with the dark teal bubbling goo which smelled of cooking meat.

Ash wrinkled his nose. Being a vegetarian, burning meat was not exactly Ash's favorite smell.

"Come here Ash," Jacob instructed.

Ash walked over and peered into the cauldron.

Shima stepped up to Ash and presented a dagger in her hands.

Ash accepted it and held it in his hand, feeling how light it was.

"Now," Jacob instructed as he rolled up Ash's sleeve, "You are going to cut your wrist and let some blood fall into the caldron as I read the spell."

Ash nodded.

Shima resumed standing by the wall, holding a stack of towels in preparation. "Master, two minutes until midnight." She alerted Jacob.

Jacob looked at Ash. "Ready?"

Ash nodded, "As, I'll ever be."

Jacob opened a brown leather bound book and began to recite a spell in Latin.

Ash understood a few words, but he did not specialize in Latin spell castings. Ash quickly ran the blade across his wrist, wincing, and watched the blood pool at the cut and began to dribble down the side of his arm. He turned his arm over the pot and watched as a few droplets dripped into the steaming cauldron. As soon as the blood came in contact with the goo, the goo bubbled even more and steam rose off it as if someone just cranked up the heat. Jacob continued to read the spell and Ash urged his blood to continue to trickle into the goo, drop by drop. The goo bubbled more and more, eventually becoming so disturbed, it began to overflow and drip down the sides. Once Jacob finished reciting the spell, the goo became still.

Ash pulled his wrist back and put pressure on it, watching the sudden silence of the settled goo.

"Your familiar is ready," Jacob informed Ash.

Ash's time had finally come, he forgot about his cut and rolled up the sleeves of the black robe. Ash took a deep breath and plunged a hand into the goo, which was still hot as hellfire. Ash only winced, he had to do this, and he reached further into the cauldron.

Jacob looked at his watch. "Hurry. You have to seal the pact before midnight."

Ash felt around in the goo, finding nothing until his fingers traced what he thought was a shoulder. Ash quickly plunged his other hand into the goo to hook his arms under the familiar's. Throwing his whole body against the cauldron, Ash was able to pull the familiar out having to struggle against the suction of the goo to lift the body out.

Jacob watched the countdown on his wrist watch. "Thirty seconds," He warned.

Ash laid the naked familiar down upon the ground, the goo was so thick on the familiar's body. Ash could not see anything, even if he wanted to.

Shima brought forth her stack of towels and offered one to Ash to clean up the familiar's face.

Jacob examined his watch as Ash and Shima cleaned up the familiar's mouth and nose. "On my countdown," Jacob instructed as the second hand drew closer to midnight.

Ash nodded and waited, everything was in slow motion to him.

Shima backed up to where she was originally before to wait.

Jacob watched his watch for a few seconds before he looked up at Ash and nodded, signaling Ash to begin.

Ash took the dagger and dug deeper into the cut, bringing up a new pool of blood. He put his wrist to his mouth and sucked up a mouthful of his own blood.

"Three..." Jacob began the countdown.

Ash carefully picked up the head of the familiar, cradling it in his arms.

"Two..."

Ash parted the familiar's lips and pinched its nose closed.

"One!" Jacob said.

Ash kissed the lifeless body forcing his mouthful of blood down its throat.

Ash could hear the grandfather clock in the room chime midnight. Each chime rang through Ash's body, making his heart grow heavier and heavier. The twelfth chime rang and the clock fell silent.

Ash watched the poor empty husk of his familiar lay still and lifeless in his arms as the chimes slowly dwindled away. The blood did not take, leaving the soulless shell. Ash sighed, he had never been so disappointed in himself before.

Jacob looked at his nephew, disappointed as well. "We can always try again next year," Jacob said softly, rubbing Ash's shoulder comfortingly.

"I really didn't want to do this again on my nineteenth birthday." Ash sighed, looking at the lifeless familiar.

Jacob pat his nephew's back. "I'm sorry. There were probably no compatible souls available this evening."

Ash nodded and sighed, disappointed. "I suppose you're right."

"Shima, take care of the body," Jacob ordered.

Shima's red eyes turned red and black and she carefully removed the familiar's body from Ash's arms. She tenderly held the soulless body, wishing like everyone else that a soul bounded to the body.

Ash stood and began cleaning up the teal goo on the floor of the potion room with his Uncle.

Shima held the body and carried it upstairs to bury it outside.

Suddenly, it gulped.

Shima gasped surprised and almost dropped the familiar. She watched in amazement as the familiar took another shaky breath. "Master! Ash!"

Ash ran over as quickly as he could and took over from Shima, holding his familiar. "It took!" Ash excitedly yelled to his Uncle. Ash watched the familiar as it unsteadily began to breathe.

Shima smiled softly and Jacob gave a triumphant grin.

Jacob looked at Shima, giving her some orders. "Take the familiar away clean it, clothe it, and lay it to rest in its new bedroom."

"Yes, Master." She bowed and then bowed to Ash. "May I take your familiar to be cleaned up?"

Ash was in shock, it took him a while to register what Shima was talking about. "Y-yeah," Ash said softly, not sure if he was truly ready to let go of his new familiar yet.

Shima carried the familiar out.

The goo was still so thickly crusted on the familiar, making it difficult to even tell what gender it was. But presently, all Ash cared about was that it was alive and breathing easily.

Chapter 3

    Trisha walked through Amington High's halls alone, on her way to the to the pick-up/drop-off area located at the front of the school. She just finished playing a volleyball game against Eastgate high. It was a close match, but Amington pulled ahead to take the final set and win the game. Trisha was sweaty and wore her practice clothes consisting of red gym shorts, a black tank top, and tennis shoes with all of her curly hair ponied on the top of her head. The rest of her clothes were in a gym bag, stuffed into her backpack. When she turned a corner, a beautiful melody caught her ear's attention. The melody was lovely and she curiously investigated where the sound was coming as she followed the melody to the band room. Trisha carefully peeked in and watched Nic stand at the front of the class practicing on his violin.

    Nic seemed like he was in a different world whenever he played an instrument. He always wore a soft smile with his eyes half closed. Nic finished the melody he was playing and Mrs. Solong, the music teacher, clapped to applaud her ace student. "Very good Nicholas, but you seem distracted," She mentioned.

    "Well...," Nic looked over at the doorway to see Trisha. He smiled at her, noticing for the first time that Trisha was standing there.

    Mrs. Solong turned around to see what Nic was grinning at. Trisha quickly ducked behind a tuba case to hide from the teacher. Mrs. Solong hated non-band students coming into the band room and Trisha had a track record of breaking that rule.

Seeing nothing, Mrs. Solong returned to lecture Nic. "You need to forget all of your distractions for the next week."

As Mrs. Solong carried on at Nic, Trisha remained hidden. She took off her backpack and removed a sketch book and a graphite pencil from within it. Trisha flipped her sketchbook open to an empty page.

Mrs. Solong was still lecturing as Trisha began sketching. "The recital this coming Friday needs your utmost attention. Your timing was off and you need to..." Nic zoned out as Mrs. Solong lectured him on things he botched or needed to improve before next Friday. Nic had a long day and double duty violin practice was doing nothing to help his nerves about the recital. "Once again and then we will call it quits." Mrs. Solong said

"Yes, ma'am." Nic responded and readied his violin.

Mrs. Solong gave a slight nod, signaling for Nic to begin.

Trisha watched Nic as he played, every part of Nic was focused on his music. His fingers touched each cord sensibly as the bow glided across the strings. Nic's soft smile and half-closed eyes were focused on the violin temporarily. Trisha paid attention to detail and added it into her sketch.

Nic's melody eventually came to an end and Mrs. Solong applauded.

Trisha about did too but stopped quickly before she could.

Nic watched Trisha carefully peek out from behind the tuba case.

After Mrs. Solong finished applauding, she called it a day. Nic began to pack up, sneaking peaks at Trisha who was focusing on her sketchbook.

"Be sure to practice over the weekend." Mrs. Solong reminded Nic for the umpteenth time.

"Yes, ma'am. I'll work on it." Nic promised the music teacher and finished packing up as Mrs. Solong lectured about the types of basics he needed to practice over the weekend and what fundamentals needed to be critiqued to better his performance.

Nic glanced up and saw Trisha fully concentrating on her sketch pad. "Have a nice weekend Mrs. Solong."

"You too Nic. Practice. Practice. Practice." She smiled, encouraging him.

Nic laughed, "I will." Nic waved bye and walked up the stairs of the auditorium-like classroom seating. Nic glanced out the corner of his eye and saw Mrs. Solong disappear into her office. He paused at the tuba case and looked down at Trisha, who was still sketching. "Are you coming?" Nic asked, offering his hand to Trisha.

Trisha looked up and accepted the help to her feet.

Mrs. Solong exited her office and Trisha ran out of the band room before she could be seen by the teacher.

Nic followed her out, laughing. "That was smooth, like crunchy peanut butter."

"Don't be mean," Trisha said softly, smiling at his joke.

Nic laughed and walked with her down the halls. "You're lucky she didn't catch you."

"I know, lunch detention for a week." Trisha sighed at the memory of a time Mrs. Solong did catch her at one of Nic's piano recitals.

Nic stopped at his locker and dropped his books off for the weekend and collected everything he needed for homework. "Did you win?"

"Huh?" She asked, not hearing him the first time.

Nic closed his locker, "Your game, did you win?" He repeated himself as the two walked down the halls.

"Oh yeah, we gave them a beating," She answered with a smile.

The two walked out the back doors of the school, into the brisk fall air.

"That's great." Nic said and noticed Trisha shivering in her t-shirt and gym shorts.

"Do you need my jacket?" Nic asked, prepared to take it off.

"No. I'll be fine," Trisha said, crossing her arms to keep the air off them.

"Are you sure?" Nic asked.

"Yes, I'm..." Trisha paused as Nic set down his violin case and took off his backpack so he could remove his black jacket.

Nic handed Trisha the jacket. "I'm not the one in shorts." He smiled, still wearing his long sleeve overshirt with a t-shirt underneath and jeans.

Trisha looked at it and blushed, her face turning the color of her gym shorts.

"You might as well wear it because I'm not putting it back on," Nic smirked, knowing he had her trapped.

Trisha took the jacket. "Are you sure?" She asked timidly, once again.

Nic sighed and helped her put the jacket on.

The jacket came down low on Trisha almost like a dress and the sleeves were too big, covering her hands.

"You look like a toddler." Nic teased his best friend after seeing the final product.

Trisha looked at the ground not sure on how to take that.

"You look cute," Nic assured her.

Warmth spread over her cheeks as she once again blushed, thankful that it was getting dark and the lighting was bad.

Nic picked his backpack and violin case up. "The plans are still on for tomorrow right? You wanted to see that chick flick still?"

"Yeah," Trisha admitted, "But we don't have to go. I thought you didn't like those types of movies."

"They aren't my favorite, but I still like them." Nic shrugged. "I want to go if you want to go. You do still want to go, right?" Nic asked, uncertain.

"Yes." Trisha gave a brief confirmation nod with her answer.

"Awesome. I'll pick you up at six." Nic smiled and pulled out an Amington University lanyard with his car keys attached to it.

"I'll be ready," Trisha promised. "Oh! And I'll give you back your jacket tomorrow."

"Sounds good. See you tomorrow." Nic waved bye and walked out to the single car left in the student parking lot.

Trisha watched him leave. "Bye," She whispered softly, giving him a small wave which he could not see as he walked away. Trisha strolled over and sat on a metal bench, pulling out her phone to call her mother. She pulled up the long sleeves of the jacket and paused. Carefully, Trisha breathed in the smelled the sleeve of the jacket.

It smelled like Nic. Nic always smelled so good, like cinnamon.

As she dialed her mother, Trisha kept the sleeve to her nose to breathe in Nic's warm scent.

Nic walked to his car in the empty parking lot and unlocked it. He threw his backpack and violin case into the backseat and closed the door. Nic glanced up at Trisha still sitting on the bench under the metal awning.

Trisha's car was still in the shop and would be for another week until the company can replace the part that was recently damaged. While work was being done on Trisha's car, her mother or father had to come to the school to pick her up and drop her off.

Nic cupped his hands around his mouth and yelled. "I can take you home!"

Trisha perked up. "Really?" She asked, yelling back.

"Wait there. I'm coming to pick you up!" Nic got in his car and cranked the engine. He pulled up to the drop-off/pick-up center where she was waiting.

Trisha opened the passenger car door. "Are you sure?" She asked shyly.

"Hop in." Nic motioned for her to get in as he busily turned down his music and began to clean up his car a bit for the beautiful passenger he was about to take home.

Trisha set her stuff cautiously in the backseat and got into Nic's car. "Thank you. The game ended earlier than I expected and my parents aren't answering their cell phones. Are you sure that you don't mind?" Trisha asked again.

"I really don't mind," Nic said. "Besides, it's not too far out of the way, what are friends for?"

Trisha buckled up and played with a loose curl. "Thanks."

"It's no problem," Nic assured her, shifting the car out of park as he pulled out of the parking lot.

For a while, all was silent, except for the hum of rock music from the radio which was turned to one of the lowest volume settings and the whirr of the heater.

Trisha pulled out her sketch pad and worked on some finishing touch ups to her most recent sketch.

Nic glanced over at what she was doing.

Trisha lifted up the edge of the sketchbook so Nic could not see.

"That's not fair." Nic laughed. "I want to see."

"No, you don't." Trisha muttered, not really focusing on Nic, but on her drawing.

Nic smirked. "It's me, isn't it?"

Trisha blushed. "No, what would give you that idea? Get over yourself." She giggled as she penciled the final details of Nic's eyes.

"Why won't you let me see then? You always use to show me your drawings." Nic reminded her.

"That was back in middle school, though," Trisha argued quietly.

"And?"

"Middle school is a weird place."

"Touché." Nic laughed.

"Mrs. Solong has never kept you in for so long before," Trisha said, trying to start a new conversation to get Nic's mind off her art.

Nic nodded, "I see what you're trying to do, Miss Distract-Him-With-A-Different-Topic-Because-He-Has-A-Short-Attention-Span."

Trisha covered her mouth and laughed. "You know me so well. But really, that scholarship recital thing has gotten both of you frazzled."

Nic laughed and nodded again, "I would be lying if I didn't say I was nervous."

"You will be fine. You really don't need to practice; you are going to do great." Trisha praised.

"Hopefully," Nic muttered.

"What do you mean?" Trisha asked, looking up from her drawing and resting her pencil behind her ear.

"I fear that I'm going to choke and it's going to be on something so simple which will completely destroy my chances with the College Board executives," Nic admitted.

"No, you're going to be awesome." Trisha encouraged. "When you win the scholarship, are you going to attend Amington University?"

"If I win," Nic corrected, "Then yes. Amington has a nice music program and I would like to continue." Nic glanced over at Trisha as he drove before returning his attention back to the road. "What universities have you applied to?"

"Tempton University, Univesity of Winchest, and Eastgate University."

Nic whistled, those are all pretty big league schools. "Wow. With your grades and test scores, you should be able to get in with no problem." Nic assured her.

"There's only one school for me, though," Trisha said softly, pulling up her sketchbook to try and hide behind it as she waited for Nic to catch the hints she was laying out for him.

"What do you mean?" Nic asked, confused as her hint flew over his head.

"I want to go where you go." Trisha tried again, almost too nervous to say it.

"Amington is an art school, but it's still good. It has several nice programs." Nic said, still not getting the big picture.

Trisha sighed quietly and looked out the window, wondering if all boys were as dense as Nic.

Nic's car pulled up to a red light and stopped. With the light red at the busy intersection, Nic reached into the middle console of his car and pulled out a little pale blue box. "I swear if you had just waited until tomorrow, I would have done this formally with a movie and dinner. But since you were so insistent," Nic smiled and gave Trisha the tiny blue box, "Happy birthday."

"W-what?" Trisha asked confused, looking at the tiny box.

"I won't be able to make it to your birthday this coming Friday with the scholarship recital and I feel horrible. So I wanted to celebrate your birthday tomorrow." Nic shrugged like it was no big deal.

"R-really?" Trisha asked in shock, finding it getting a little stuffy in Nic's car.

"Yes really. Now open your gift." Nic demanded, more than requested.

Trisha smiled and opened the little box to show a sterling silver promise ring. Her jaw dropped and her eyes widened; the ring was beautiful.

"Do you like it?" Nic asked.

"I love it, but… I can't accept this." Trisha admitted looking at the little ring.

"Why not?" Nic asked, confused.

"It's too much," Trisha answered, putting the lid back on the box containing the ring.

"What do you mean?" Nic asked as he watched Trisha pack her gift away to return to him.

"Nic, this is typically stuff boyfriends and girlfriends get each other," Trisha explained.

"And?" Nic asked.

"And what? We aren't dating, so this is too much." Trisha rationalized.

"Trisha," Nic blushed. "I was going to ask you out tomorrow," He admitted.

Trisha blushed, "Y-you were?"

"Yeah, I was going to do it during dinner. But well… uh, now you know." Nic shrugged, trying to make it sound like it was no big deal. But on the inside, he felt like his organs were turning to mush.

Trisha removed the lid of her present and looked back at the ring, smiling. She gently punched Nic in the arm like she did earlier. "Dummy, if you liked me that way, you should've asked me sooner. You didn't have to wait until my birthday."

Nic rubbed his arm and smiled, "My mistake."

Trisha rolled her eyes and placed a tender kiss on Nic's cheek. "Yes."

"Huh?" Nic asked, dazed by the sudden kiss.

"Yes, I will go out with you." She clarified, taking the ring back out of its box.

Nic's blush darkened as he touched his cheek where she kissed him.

Trisha slipped the promise ring onto her finger as the red light turned green.

Nic pulled out into the intersection and everything seemed like it was in slow motion.

A car ran its red light at the busy intersection and crashed into the driver's side of Nic's car, flipping it.

#####

Trisha slowly opened her eyes and looked around. It eventually dawned on her that she was hanging upside down by the way her hair fell up and how her sketchbook was resting on the ceiling. A gash on Trisha's forehead dripped blood onto the sketchbook's exposed pages. Dust was flying everywhere coating the inside of her throat and stinging her eyes. Trisha did not know if it was her busted forehead or the hanging upside down bit, but she was quickly becoming lightheaded. She reached for her seatbelt but had no strength in her body to try to unfasten it.

    The car door was forced open and someone shined a light from their cell phone into the car. A Hispanic woman was kneeling with the phone wearing scrubs with a cartoon dog on it as an older man in a business suit held the door open. The Hispanic woman was speaking to Trisha informing her that she was a registered nurse and that 911 was on the way. But Trisha could not focus, distracted by a constant ringing in her ear making her tune out what the nurse was saying.

    Trisha looked at the lady, nothing was making sense to her. The crash had happened so quickly that Trisha never saw the other car which hit them. She returned to trying to unbuckle the seatbelt with no success.

    The older man supported Trisha as the Hispanic woman reached past the teen to unbuckle the seatbelt for her.

    Delicately, the man lowered Trisha down onto the ground so she could crawl out. Once on the ground, Trisha looked at Nic and her eyes widened in horror.

    Nic's body was in a horrible position with his head twisted to the side. Nic's face was bloody from broken glass and debris. The teen was pinned into his car, barely able to breathe from the steering wheel crushing his chest.

    "N-N-Nic?" Trisha asked, trembling as she gently reached out and touched his arm.

    Nic's eyes slowly opened and they looked around to find Trisha, trying to get his bearing from hanging upside down as well. He opened his mouth to say something, but blood poured out spilling into his eyes and down his forehead.

Trisha screamed and the older man helped pull Trisha from the car. Trisha laid on the asphalt, shaking as tears streamed down her cheeks as she hugged Nic's jacket to her body. "Help... please." She whispered a plea. "Help him."

The registered nurse tended to Trisha's injuries using a first aid kit from her car as an ambulance finally arrived on scene followed by police officers and fire trucks. The firefighters approached the car and used a machine to wrench the door open. "N-Nic... accident... oh my god!" Trisha stammered, breaking down into tears as EMT's ran over to the car with a stretcher.

Trisha looked across the road to see the other car, its bumper was completely destroyed, but other than that the car was fine. A girl stood beside her car talking to a police officer. Trisha recognized her from class, it was Jessica Norton.

A bystander walked over to offer assistance and to check on Trisha, but the Hispanic nurse piped up first, "Do you know what happened?"

The bystander nodded. "Apparently the girl was texting her boyfriend and driving."

A knot was growing in Trisha's throat as she watched the firefighters struggle to get Nic out from behind the steering wheel.

With a snap, the firefighters were able to tear the steering wheel completely off for the EMTs to skillfully maneuver Nic out of the pinned confines of his car. The

EMTs strapped Nic to a stretcher and attached an oxygen mask to his face as they ran Nic over to an ambulance.

Trisha tried to stand but she was so dizzy. "I want to go with him."

"No sweetie." The Hispanic woman said softly wrapping an arm around the girl's shoulders to comfort her. "They need to get him to the hospital as fast as they can without any distractions."

Trisha watched as the EMTs closed the doors of the ambulance and pulled away with the sirens blaring.

#####

The EMTs strapped Nic to several machines.

"He is going into hypovolemic shock." A female EMT alerted the other EMT.

"Signs of neck, spinal, cranial, and internal trauma." The male EMT analyzed Nic's vitals.

"Blood pressure is 103 over 89 and decreasing. Pulse rate is 126 BPM."

The male EMT shined a light into Nic's eyes. "We're losing him."

As the two EMTs talked, Nic listened to everything they were saying. Nic did not feel any pain; he even felt warm, comfortable, and peaceful. Nic had seen Trisha crying and wanted to tell her that it was okay, he was alive and fine. But was he really? Surely car crashes had to hurt, so why was he in no pain? He smiled softly and closed his eyes as he let the warm feeling overtake him.

Chapter 4

White was the first thing Nic saw when he opened his eyes. He looked up at a white ceiling with a white ceiling fan that was slowly spinning in a hypnotic circle. Nic coughed, irritating his dry throat. He looked to his right and saw white walls with a closet door open revealing an assortment of clothes inside. The only furniture in the room was a bed and a wooden dresser against the opposing wall; to his left was a door fully opened to reveal a bathroom.

Nic slowly sat up, wondering where he was. The room did not look like a hospital room and he was not wearing a green backless hospital gown either. He wore a black t-shirt with gray slumber pants and as Nic looked his body over, he could not help but notice that there were no bandages either. Of all the things, Nic's nails caught his attention; they appeared like they were painted black. Nic carefully tried to scratch the paint off with his fingernail, but nothing was scrapping off.

Nic looked around the room one more time before pushing back the comforter of the bed and slowly standing. He supported himself against the wall, feeling very weak. But he had to find out what was going on. He slowly made his way to the bathroom.

His throat was so dry he could not swallow. He needed to drink something, he was so thirsty.

Nic ambled over to the sink and turned on the faucet. He stuck his head underneath and gulped mouthfuls of water; but no matter how much he drank, he was still parched. He washed his face and looked into the mirror. Nic stared frozen in place as he looked at a complete stranger staring back at him in the mirror.

The teen staring back at Nic had hair as black as a raven's wing. It was short and messy from sleeping on it. The teen was also ghostly pale and shaking slightly from exhaustion. But the most shocking feature were the reflection's eyes, blood was all Nic could think of to describe the color of the eyes that stared back at him.

"Wh-what's going on?" He hoarsely asked no one in particular, his tongue tripping up over his teeth. Nic carefully opened his mouth to expose canines which had elongated and become sharper, almost like fangs. He carefully took his index finger and touched one, pricking his finger with the slightest bit of pressure. Instead of red blood, teal goo formed at the prick wound. Before his eyes, Nic watched as the prick healed superhumanly quick.

Weirded out, Nic supported himself against the bathroom counter, shaking. He staggered out of the bathroom to the door which Nic assumed led out of the room. He fumbled with the doorknob until it finally opened it. Nic peaked out the door into a hallway. He looked down the hallway and stepped out of the bedroom. "Hello?" He asked, trying to find anyone. He needed to know what was going on.

There was no answer.

Nic stayed close to the wall as he journeyed down the hallway. The house must be huge given the size of the hallway and with the house so sophistically decorated, he felt like he was in some sort of castle. Wherever he was and whatever was going on, Nic was going to find out.

#####

Shima carried her skillet and a pot of coffee to the dining table where Ash sat with his Uncle. Jacob sipped coffee from a cup as he read the newspaper. "Blueberry pancake?" Shima asked Ash, noticing his plate was getting low.

"Yes please," Ash said, letting Shima place a fresh pancake on his plate.

"Anything for you Master?" Shima offered, approaching Jacob.

"Coffee." Jacob said never looking up from his paper, but holding up the cup.

"Yes, Master." She smiled and filled the cup up. Once her duty was momentarily fulfilled, she returned to the kitchen, but stopped at the doorway of the dining room and gasped almost dropping her pot of coffee.

The two wizards looked up, hearing the familiar's surprised reaction.

Standing before Shima was the new familiar, blocking the doorway to the dining room. The new familiar was panting and shaking from exhaustion. He was paler than a typical familiar and completely soaked in sweat.

"You are not supposed to be out of bed yet." Shima lectured the familiar, waving her spatula at him.

Like all familiars, the teenager had blood red eyes and black hair, which hung short and messy from just waking up.

Ash stood and walked over to the boy. Ash was a little taller than the familiar, but they looked about the same age.

The familiar squinted his eyes like he was trying to see something and focus on it. "Ash?" He asked hoarsely.

"Yes. I'm Ash, do I know you?" Ash asked the familiar.

The familiar's body trembled and Ash supported the familiar as his legs started to give out from underneath him. "Wow. I got ya." Ash said, holding the familiar up.

Jacob rushed over and helped Ash support the weak familiar. "He needs sleep and nourishment. The body is still trying to reject the soul."

Ash slipped the familiar's arm over his shoulder and supported him, so he could walk him back upstairs. Even through the pajamas, Ash could feel the burning fever on his familiar's skin.

Jacob helped carry Ash's familiar back to the bedroom that the familiar woke in previously. The two laid the familiar in bed and delicately tucked him in.

Jacob laughed. "A bit of a handful isn't he?"

"Yeah..." Ash said distantly.

Jacob sensed Ash's vague hesitation. "What's wrong?" He asked.

"The familiar knew my name," Ash mentioned, thinking.

"How curious...," Jacob rubbed his chin. "It seems that this familiar has a few surprises to him."

Ash nodded.

"I will bring your breakfast to you, stay with your familiar," Jacob instructed his nephew. "Make sure to feed him properly."

"Yeah, yeah," Ash muttered and sat on the edge of the bed beside his familiar as Jacob exited the room.

Ash's familiar was still conscious and looked up at him with half-lidded red eyes. The familiar coughed, his black hair stuck to his forehead in clumps. Ash stood and walked over to the dresser.

On the dresser was a black and silver box which Ash opened, inside were two daggers. Every familiar needed a weapon to defend their master and Ash had made these years ago as part of his magical training to give to his future familiar. Ash removed a single dagger from the box and walked back to the bed. He sat back down on the edge and began to unwrap the bandage he made last night for his cut wrist. With the dagger, he cautiously reopened the wound.

The smell of Ash's blood was in the air and the newborn familiar's nose instantly picked up the scent. Ash watched as the white of the familiar's red eyes were consumed by black as instinct took the familiar over. From what Jacob taught him, teaching a familiar to feed was like teaching a baby to suckle.

The familiar, looked at Ash and the blood, driven by instinct to feed but not knowing what to do.

Ash took a dab of blood on his index finger and painted his familiar's bottom lip.

It did not take the familiar long to begin licking his lips and drinking up the blood.

Ash offered his bloody wrist and placed it close to the familiar's mouth.

The familiar smelled it and carefully licked it, tasting the blood. The familiar acted more like a feral animal than a human presently.

"It's okay," Ash said softly. "You need to drink up to become strong."

The familiar licked Ash's wrist a few more times, getting a few drops of blood.

A Familiar's body has very special abilities, their spit had healing effects on the bodies of others. So, as the familiar continued to lick the cut, the wound only healed making it harder for him to drink.

The familiar gently took hold of Ash's wrist, getting braver in his actions as he licked the healing cut.

Ash winced, as the familiar finally figured out how to use his fangs to puncture the flesh to draw more blood out. The bite mark was very sloppy and the familiar dragged his fangs across the puncture wound when he withdrew them, ripping the flesh open wider than he was supposed to. Blood pumped out and the familiar drank heartily, taking as much as he needed. After drinking several mouthfuls, the familiar refused to drink anymore. He carefully licked the wound clean to heal it up. After that, the familiar let go of Ash's arm and nestled back down in bed to sleep.

Jacob came in moments later with Ash's plate and his book bag. "How did he feed?"

"Good. What now?" Ash asked, accepting his plate. Ash was completely fine after letting his familiar feed from him.

Another special ability familiars have is their 'venom' they inject into their prey. It is not really venom but more of a special type of chemical. The chemical served two functions, it prevents clots forming so they can drink without anything stopping them and it affects the bone marrow to increase red blood cell production tenfold to replenish the missing blood the familiars take almost instantaneously. The 'venom' and the healing saliva make a perfect combination for the familiars to feed without any problems to either party.

"Now you wait," Jacob answered.

"Awesome." Ash responded and turned to walk past Jacob, but was stopped in his tracks by Jacob holding him by the collar of his shirt.

"Where do you think you're going?" Jacob asked Ash.

"To wait for my familiar to wake up, preferably in my room," Ash answered.

Jacob laughed. "No. You'll wait here with your familiar."

"What am I supposed to do in the meantime then?" Ash asked, crossing his arms.

Jacob smiled and handed Ash his backpack full of schoolwork. "No time like the present to start on that pesky homework."

Ash moaned and watched Jacob leave, whole-heartedly laughing. "Damn that old man." He huffed and sat down on the bed beside the sleeping familiar to begin on the homework.

#####

The familiar's red eyes opened and he looked to his side where Ash sat reading a textbook and chewing on the eraser of his pencil.

It took Ash a while to notice that his familiar was finally awake. The familiar was just lying there, staring at Ash for a long while, dazed. The familiar's eyes were no longer consumed by black, they were back to their normal red color. The familiar also did not look as pale as he did before which was a very good sign.

"Ash? Where am I?" The familiar asked softly, his voice no longer hoarse but still weak.

There it was again, the familiar knew Ash's name somehow.

"Who are you?" Ash asked.

The familiar sat up slowly, supporting himself with his elbows.

Ash put his book down and placed a soft pillow behind the familiar's back to help him sit up without straining his new body. "Nic. We've been going to the same school forever." The familiar answered, leaning against the pillow Ash set up for him.

"Nic? Nic Russell?" Ash asked in disbelief. Nic looked nothing like how he use to with his golden blonde hair now black, green eyes now red, and his tanned complexion now pale. Ash paused as something clicked in his head. If Nic was now a familiar, that meant that since school yesterday he had to have...

"What happened?" Nic asked; he was still a bit dazed from everything.

"What do you remember?" Ash asked, not knowing where to even begin to ease Nic into this.

"There was a car accident. A car hit me on the driver side when I was taking Trisha home. I think I blacked out. Where's Trisha? Is she okay?" Nic asked, concerned and forced himself to sit up.

Ash eased Nic back down to rest against the pillows. "Trisha isn't here."

"Where am I?" Nic asked, looking around and noticing that he was back in the white room where had originally started.

"You're in your new room at your new residence."

"I don't understand." Nic threw the sheets off. "Where are my clothes? I need my cell phone. It's in my pants pocket." Nic said and weakly climbed out of bed.

"You need to get back in bed," Ash advised. "Shima says that you shouldn't be up and about right now."

"No, I need to talk to Trisha. I have to see if she's okay." Nic said, refusing to listen to Ash.

Ash sighed and looked at Nic. "I'm sorry. I wasn't expecting to start doing this until later." He muttered under his breath. He took a deep breath and looked at Nic. "Nic, I order you to get back into bed," Ash commanded, issuing an absolute order.

Nic glared at Ash, suddenly his eyes shifted color. Black enveloped everything but the red irises and Nic could no longer control his body. As ordered, Nic crawled back into bed and pulled the sheets over his body to tuck himself in. "What the hell?" Nic muttered struggling, trying to fight against the order.

"A wizard's word is binding to his familiar. I have some explaining to do," Ash said. "Now you're going to shut up and listen, okay?"

After no response from Nic, Ash crossed his arms. "Am I understood?"

Nic's eyes widened with terror as he felt two words flow over his tongue, Nic clenched his teeth and tried to swallow the words from coming up like vomit. But no matter how much he tried to hold those two words back they came out with full force, letting Ash hear the words clearly.

"Yes, Master."

Chapter 5

"So, let me get this perfectly clear," Nic said, still under Ash's orders to lay in bed and rest. "I died yesterday in that car accident?"

"Yes," Ash said, shuffling a card deck as he sat beside Nic.

"You're a wizard who can do all this magic stuff and on your eighteenth birthday you made a...?" Nic paused forgetting the technical term.

"Familiar." Ash filled in the blank.

"A familiar," Nic continued, "Which are beings that are basically slaves to witches and wizards."

Ash shrugged, it was a rough definition but close enough.

"I'm a familiar and familiars cannot be seen by humans." Nic finished.

"Unless in your animal form." Ash corrected Nic.

Nic only looked at Ash and struggled once again to get out of bed. An invisible force acted upon Nic like someone had tied a rope around his body, and it refused to let him move. Nic cried out frustrated. "There is no such thing as magic!" Nic yelled, he could not take any more of this nonsense. "I'm just having a drug induced dream. I'm going to wake up soon in the hospital, and I'll be in a lot of pain. But Trisha will be there," Nic argued in denial.

Ash thought for a second and stood. He looked through Nic's closet and found a warm jacket and threw it over his shoulder. He walked back over to Nic and brushed some black locks of hair out of the way and gently felt Nic's forehead. Nic's fever was broken, but he still could use the bed rest. "You may get out of bed, but be gentle on your body." Ash expelled the order.

Nic slowly sat up, still a bit weak.

Ash threw the jacket into the familiar's lap. "You may want to put that on," Ash advised.

"Huh?" Nic asked, picking up the jacket and holding it.

"You want to see for yourself what's going on, right?" Ash asked.

Nic nodded slowly, "Yeah."

"Well, follow me," Ash said solemnly, walking out.

Nic jumped out of bed, throwing his jacket on as he followed Ash.

#####

Ash drove Nic to Amington emergency hospital and parked in the visitor parking garage. The two walked to the hospital emergency room and entered.

The two looked around, for a Saturday it was not too busy. Ash glanced at Nic standing beside him and motioned for him to go up to the counter and talk to the receptionist. Ash took a seat in a chair and picked up a dated magazine.

Nic looked around the emergency room. He knew that he must have looked odd, Nic did not even think of changing before leaving Ash's house. Not only was Nic in pajamas with only a thin jacket on, but he was barefoot too. Even though Nic knew that he must have looked ridiculous, no one was looking at him. Nic strode up to the receptionist. "E-Excuse me," Nic said timidly. He paused and mentally kicked himself, why was he being timid? Nic cleared his throat, he had business to discuss. "Excuse me," Nic repeated with more power and strength behind his voice.

Anyone would have looked up or even acknowledged Nic's presence, but the lady did nothing. She continued to type on her keyboard as she popped bubble gum and looked at her computer screen. "Excuse me!" Nic snapped at her, getting a little pissed at how rude she was being. But he was still met with only silence and no sign of any type of response from the nurse. "I'm standing right in front of you dammit!" Nic yelled and his fist hit the counter making a cup of pens spill.

The woman gasped surprised, looking at the mess of scattered pens.

"Finally," Nic sighed in relief as the woman began to pick up the pens strewn across her desk. "My name is Nicholas Russell. I was in a car accident yesterday with my girlfriend, Trisha Roxwell."

The woman put the cup full of pens back on the counter and continued typing on her computer, never hearing Nic, as she popped her gum.

"Hello?" Nic tried again.

Ash looked up from the magazine and sighed, this could take all day.

A man approached the counter where Nic was attempting to talk to the receptionist and walked right through Nic.

Nic jumped back and touched his chest, eyes wide in shock.

The nurse took the man's paperwork and the man returned to sit down, walking back through Nic.

Nic shakily looked at his hands.

Ash sighed and set his magazine down. He stood up and walked over, "Do you understand now?" He asked softly, under his breath.

Nic could not admit it, he refused to believe. He only stared forward in shock.

"May I help you, hun?" The receptionist asked Ash who stood right beside Nic.

Ash looked at Nic and sighed. "Actually, I was hoping if you would know if Trisha Roxwell checked in yesterday? She was in a terrible car accident last night." Ash explained approaching the counter.

The administrative nurse typed a few things into her computer. "Yes, but she already checked out earlier this morning."

"How was she?" Ash asked.

"Well enough to check out apparently." The receptionist replied.

"That's good, what about the driver? It was a boy named Nic Russell."

The nurse sighed, not needing to type anything into the computer. "God rest his soul. He checked in yesterday as well, he was on life support and barely made in through the front door before he flat-lined. I think they took him straight to the morgue after that."

Nic's chest was tightening and a ball was forming in his throat that he could not swallow.

"Thank you. That helped a lot." Ash smiled sadly. He walked out the sliding front doors and Nic followed. "Believe me now?" Ash asked under his breath, not wanting to be seen talking to no one.

"I need proof. I can't be dead," Nic refused to believe until he saw with his own eyes.

"Dude! No one can see you, you obviously have memories of dying, you keep denying the reason you are back yet I am the only one who can see you, and somebody just walked through you dammit! How much more proof do you need?!" Ash yelled at Nic, momentarily losing his short temper.

A few EMTs standing outside their ambulance in the emergency departure sector looked over at Ash as he yelled at his invisible cohort on the public sidewalk.

"You okay buddy?" An EMT asked, concerned.

"Yep! A- Okay. Everything is fine. Nothing is wrong with me, I promise. Sorry for disturbing you!" Ash smiled and turned to walk away, he glared at Nic. "See? People think I'm crazy if I talk to you." Ash muttered under his breath as they walked back to his car.

Nic walked with Ash, looking back over his shoulder at the hospital periodically.

Ash groaned seeing Nic so sad and lethargic. He grabbed Nic's wrist and pulled him behind some shrubbery.

Nic let out a surprised yelp and crouched beside Ash, as they hid in some bushes. "What are you doing?" Nic whispered.

"First off no one can see or hear you, so you don't have to whisper," Ash whispered. "And secondly, you're my familiar. If you will not be happy until you have proof, it's my job to show you proof." Ash pulled a thick deck of cards out from a side pocket in his cargo pants.

"I highly doubt a card game will count as proof." Nic sighed.

"Shut up." Ash hissed. "I'm trying to help you."

"How?" Nic asked.

"I am a wizard who specializes in cards," Ash replied, shuffling the deck of cards in his hands.

"Cards?" Nic raised an eyebrow.

"Yes," Ash answered, "Some specialize through wands, potions, talismans, hexes, charms, and so on; but I specialize in cards."

Nic was very skeptical and gave Ash a look that said, 'yeah, right'.

Ash glared at Nic, "Just watch." With his middle and index finger, Ash tapped the top of the card deck. "Bring forth 'Blinding Mist'." He pulled a card out of the deck randomly and showed it to Nic.

The card showed some monsters trapped in a cloud; on the card it read 'Blinding Mist'.

"Hey, wait," Nic said, taking the card from his master to look at it. "Isn't that a card from that stupid role-playing game at school?"

Ash rolled his eyes. "It's not a stupid role playing game, it's called Spellcaster. And just for your information, it is the best RPG known to mankind." Ash argued, taking his card back. "And be careful with my cards, they are collectors editions."

"Uh-huh..." Nic smirked. "And I bet you wonder why girls don't flock to you."

"Shut up," Ash ordered.

The white of Nic's red eyes were consumed by black as the order took control. Nic found that he could not even open his mouth. Nic wanted to yell at Ash, but he remained silent and crossed his arms as he waited for the order to be rescinded.

Ash lifted the card of 'Blinding Mist' and whispered, "Activate." The magic word made his card vanish with a bright light. Ash climbed out of the bush and offered his hand to Nic, pulling the familiar out as well.

The two walked back into the hospital, passing the EMTs on the way in.

Ash nudged Nic in the side, "Watch this."

Nic watched Ash jump onto a waiting table and yell. "Hello, Amington!"

Nic averted his eyes before remembering that he could not be seen, but Ash could.

Yet no one looked at the wizard, no one in the waiting room even seemed bothered.

Ash jumped off the table, laughing.

Nic shook his hands wanting to say something, but the order for his silence was too strong.

Ash was confused by Nic's random arm gestures. "Say something."

Nic gasped finding his mouth could open once again. "What are you doing?!"

Ash shrugged, "Seeing if my magic worked."

"And if it didn't?" Nic asked, looking around.

"Well, security would already be here." Ash rationalized, scratching his cheek with a finger as he thought.

Nic looked at Ash stupefied for a second and then started to laugh.

Ash was surprised by Nic's reaction. "You okay?"

"I'm fine." Nic laughed and conquered his laughing fit. "You're still reckless, I see."

Ash smirked. "Thanks. I find that it's a good quality I have perfected on since my childhood. Now follow me." Ash unknowingly ordered again.

"Like I have a choice," Nic muttered, his eyes shifting to become black. He quickly followed Ash through a door which read 'authorized personnel only'.

The pair walked down some stairs which lead to the basement. They followed directory signs to the morgue and found it, but the door was only accessible with a security pass.

"Damn it," Nic muttered.

Ash looked at Nic with a raised eyebrow. "You really still doubt me?" He asked and pulled out his deck of Spellcaster cards. Ash touched the top of the deck, "Bring forth 'Hijack Device'." Ash pulled a card out of the deck and it was the 'Hijack Device' card he needed. "Activate," The word made the card glow with magic.

Ash quickly ran the card through the security scan. The light on the door beeped red twice before turning green and unlocking.

"Release, 'Hijack Device'," The card's light disappeared and Ash returned the card back to the deck before opening the door.

The two entered the morgue, and Nic immediately scrunched his nose. The hospital smelled bad like disinfectant, but the morgue was even worse. A familiar's body had heightened senses, so his sense of smell was about ten times more powerful than the average human. Nic held a hand over his nose as he entered, the smell of death and disinfectant was blending together in a nauseating stench making his stomach churn.

Ash walked over to a desk and looked at the paperwork piled on it. He carefully picked up a record with Nic's name scrawled across the top.

Nic looked around the morgue. There were empty autopsy tables, cabinets filled with medical supplies and chemicals, and a fridge where some organs sat in labeled tupperware containers; it was disgusting.

"Name: Nicholas Tanner Russell. Age: 18. Time of Death: 7:48 pm. Date of Death: November 12th. Cause of death: Blood loss. Additional notes," Ash whistled.

"What?" Nic asked, walking over to examine the report about himself.

"Additional notes included other injuries such as collapsed lungs, broken neck, internal bleeding, ruptured organs," Ash scanned the list. "Damn your list goes on forever." Ash looked up at a wall of metal doors where the dead bodies were stored. Ash looked at Nic's file and noted how all the doors had a number engraved into them. "You're in number four," Ash informed Nic as they looked for the correct door. "Ah, there you are," Ash said, finding the metal door with a four engraved into it. Ash handed Nic the file, "Hold this; I've always wanted to do this." Ash rolled up the sleeves of his black jacket and opened the metal door.

A strong scent hit Nic's nose making his stomach churn violently. He slapped his nose and turned away from the door.

Ash glanced over at Nic, noticing the familiar was paler than usual. "You okay? You look a little sick."

"I'm fine." Nic coughed, leaning against an autopsy table for support.

Ash, not bothered by the smell, continued to pull out the gurney holding Nic's body.

Nic looked at himself for the longest time before he could process that he was actually looking at himself. It was odd and he could not look away from his lifeless body.

"Proof enough?" Ash asked with an eyebrow raised.

Nic's human body looked horrible. He was deathly pale and cuts littered his body from the broken glass in his car. Nic's broken body was completely naked, but someone put a small towel over his lower body, trying to cover him up somewhat with his manhood concealed underneath. Nic's face was covered in cuts and his neck was at an awkward angle, the telltale signs that it was broken very close to the base of his head. Nic's stomach was black and bloated, filled with blood and other fluids from the ruptured organs within the body. The last shocking aspect was his left leg which was basically snapped in two, giving a clear view of the bone in the broken leg.

The longer Nic looked, the sicker he became. He covered his mouth once again and rushed over to the sink by the autopsy table.

Ash heard Nic retch into the sink as he examined Nic's body. The blonde haired, green-eyed teen was the pride and joy of the school, and now he was gone. It happened so fast, like blowing out a candle. Ash looked over at Nic, who was trying to vomit but nothing was coming up.

Ash walked over and patted Nic's shoulder. "You okay?" Ash asked, and gently rubbed small circles on Nic's back to try and comfort the familiar.

"I-I don't feel so good." Nic admitted, white knuckling the sink.

"I should've waited until you we stronger to bring you here, you're only just a changeling after all."

Nic whipped his mouth. "I want to go home."

"As you wish," Ash said, walking back over to Nic's body.

"Can we put me…uh… him… uh… it back now?" Nic asked.

Ash contemplated for a second and looked Nic in the eyes. "No."

Nic was shocked by Ash's unpredicted answer. "Why not?" Nic asked confused.

"I want you to tell me that you believe. I want you to swear it and mean it. And we aren't leaving until you do so and full heartedly mean it." Ash said, crossing his arms and leaning against the doctor's desk. "This is not an order; I want you to willingly say this."

Anger welled up within Nic, why did he have to bend to Ash's wants and needs? "Fine."

"No. I want to hear the words." Ash insisted.

Nic heard someone come down the stairs and panicked. "Please, just put me back. Someone's coming."

"Let them come, it's not like we can be seen." Ash shrugged.

"But my body can be seen," Nic said nervously.

"Admit it and I will put your body back."

"Stop! Please put my body back!" Nic pleaded nervously, hearing the unknown person get closer and closer.

"Say it! Tell me the truth!" Ash ordered in his anger, unintentionally.

Nic's red eyes became black. Even with his eyes in that state, Ash could see tears well up. Nic looked away; confusion, anger, and fear were clashing in his mind. Nic wanted to scream his frustrations, but the truth was slipping out of him from the order. Tears fell down Nic's cheeks, unable to keep them in anymore. Nic fell to his knees, grinding his teeth, refusing the order. He trembled and he could no longer hold the words back anymore as they rushed out of his mouth like vomit. "I died in a car crash last night. I'm scared and I don't know what to do." Nic was shaking, and his eyes never met Ash's.

Ash watched Nic, feeling horrible as the familiar confessed; Nic's words were like a diary entry that no one was ever supposed to hear.

"I don't want to be a familiar! I want to live with Trisha and play my music. I want to travel the world and do something with my life. But more than anything right now, I want you to put my body back!" Nic begged.

Ash and Nic looked over to see a female doctor scan her security pass.

Ash dropped Nic's file on the floor and quickly pushed Nic's body back into the little cubby in the wall and closed the metal door just in time as the female doctor entered.

She looked around and spied Nic's file on the floor. She walked over and picked it up, wondering aloud on how it got there. She shrugged and set it on the on the desk where Ash originally found it. The female doctor checked to make sure everything was off and all the bodies were sealed in each of their individual compartments before locking up and leaving for the day.

Ash looked at Nic, who was still on the floor with tears streaming down his cheeks.

Ash sighed and got on his knees to gently hug Nic. "I'm sorry. I won't be that harsh again. I'm sorry." Ash repeated, hugging Nic. "Please don't cry, I'll feel like an even bigger jerk if you do." Ash apologized and patted his familiar's back.

"I'm not crying," Nic mumbled as he wiped his eyes, trying to hide it from Ash, "I got some antiseptic in it or something, but you are a jerk."

Ash rolled his eyes and stood. "Come on. Let's get you home." He smiled softly, offering his hand to Nic.

Nic wiped his eyes and accepted Ash's help.

Chapter 6

Nic carefully tied on a black tie and stuffed it into his vest, trying to look presentable. Nic was currently hiding in his cramped closet as Shima sat on his bed.

As soon as Nic and Ash returned home from their journey to the hospital, Jacob had whisked Ash away to practice magic and ordered Shima to begin Nic's familiar training.

Step one of familiar training is to present oneself in appropriate attire to their master.

"Are you done yet?" Shima asked, sighing. She was getting bored of waiting for the young familiar to get dressed.

"If you gave me some privacy, I wouldn't take so long," Nic informed the female familiar as he finally came out of the closet.

Nic was dressed in black slacks with a white dress shirt accompanied with a gray vest and a black tie. He rolled up the sleeves to his elbows and loosened his tie a bit to be comfortable, yet presentably well-dressed.

"Those clothes fit you well. You clean up nicely Nicky!" Shima beamed.

"Nic, I prefer Nic." He informed her and walked to the bathroom to look at himself in the mirror. Nic stared at the stranger in the mirror, still not use to his new reflection. He gently pulled on a lock of black hair and watched his reflection do the same thing.

"Think of it as a new 'Nic'-name." She giggled at her own pun and walked into the bathroom with Nic.

Nic looked at Shima in the mirror. The two familiars were about the same height, but Shima was in heels.

"A familiar's duty is to their master," Shima educated her pupil, "In exchange they feed, house, clothe, and protect us."

"Protect us?" Nic asked.

"Yes," Shima answered, fixing her hair in the mirror. "There are tons of things that can hurt us; other familiars, witches, wizards, anything that goes bump in the night really, especially grim reapers."

"Grim reapers, those exist?" Nic looked at Shima.

Shima's red eyes met Nic's. "Yes, and they are a force to be reckoned with." She coughed to change the subject. "Moving on, a familiar's job is to protect and serve our masters," Shima said, lecturing Nic. "Your first task as a familiar will be making your master a simple afternoon snack."

#####

Ash stirred a beautiful lilac purple liquid within a black cauldron.

Jacob looked at Ash's work. "How do you know when a love potion is finished?" Jacob asked his nephew.

"When it's the perfect shade of lilac purple, smells of roses, and is the consistency of milk," Ash answered, still stirring the concoction within the cauldron.

"Very good, you've been studying," Jacob observed. "Now, let's get this into some vials to sell."

"Yes, sir." Ash said and began to ladle love potion into tiny decorative crystal vials.

Shima knocked on the door of the study before entering with a tray of tea.

Nic entered after Shima, dressed like a full-fledged familiar. Nic also carried a tray, but his held coffee and a plate of cookies.

Shima walked over to Jacob and served him his afternoon tea.

Nic did the same setting a cup down for Ash and pouring coffee into it. "Do you take cream or sugar?" Nic asked.

"Neither. I take it black." Ash said picking up his cup and blowing on it before taking a sip.

"Black? Really?" Nic asked, scrunching his nose.

Ash sipped his coffee and smirked. "Yeah?"

Shima cleared her throat.

Nic sighed. "Is there anything else I can get you?" Nic said politely though it sounded like he was reading from a script.

Upon hearing those words, Shima smiled, content.

"No thanks."

Nic set down a plate with three chocolate chip cookies on it. "Then please enjoy," Nic said through clenched teeth. It was humiliating to serve Ash like this. Ash was well... he was Ash. The kid Nic went to kindergarten with, the one always sitting in the corner playing with a deck of cards.

Ash took another sip of his coffee. "Thank you."

Nic gave a courtesy nod and turned to walk out, but Shima grabbed him by the back of his collar and spun Nic back around.

"What of our chores Master?" Shima bowed her head slightly.

Jacob thought for a bit. "Our bedroom can use a cleanup."

"It will be done, my lord." Shima bowed graciously.

Nic rolled his eyes and Shima nudged him hard in the side with her elbow.

Ash saw the attitude Nic was directing more toward Shima than anyone else. As if from a script, Nic asked Ash sarcastically. "Master, what am I supposed to do all day?" Nic was just begging to piss Shima off, which he was on the brink of already.

As far as Shima was concerned, Nic was making her look bad. Shima never looked bad, definitely not in front of her Master.

Ash smirked, he found Nic quite humorous. "I'd like it if you can clean up my room, please." Ash requested, trying to show Nic that he wanted the familiar to consider himself as an equal.

Nic nodded. "The honor is all mine." He smiled sarcastically.

Shima glared at Nic and cleared her throat as he turned to walk out.

"Almost forgot," Nic said as Shima reminded him. He gave a flippant bow and walked out of the room without being dismissed.

Shima followed Nic, stopping to close the study's doors. "If you will excuse us," She smiled like nothing happened and politely shut the door.

There was a long pause of awkward silence which was quickly broken by the two familiars as they battled with words and curses down the hall.

Jacob chuckled. "Shima has got her hands full."

"Nic is a little rebellious." Ash agreed.

"A little?" Jacob asked, raising an eyebrow.

Ash raised his hands in defeat. "Okay, he's a very rebellious. What am I supposed to do about it? He's working and trying to follow the rules, but things are different now. He's just trying to adjust and that will take time."

Jacob chuckled. "I never said differently. Nic is doing well, Shima is just upset that she has to slow her pace and teach someone."

"I have confidence that he'll adjust quickly." Ash agreed with his Uncle. "Now, where were we?" Ash asked, trying to remember what he had to do with the cauldron of potion in front of him.

#####

"In all my years I have never seen such a poor excuse of a familiar," Shima said, raising her nose at Nic.

"I'm sorry. Is it the dress clothes? I can go sluttier." Nic fired back at her.

"When you are in this household you will address me as 'Teacher' and show some respect." Shima scolded as they walked down the halls.

"As if," Nic huffed and crossed his arms.

Shima led Nic to Ash's room. "I was going to help you, seeing as this is your first task and all, but I will make my case." Shima opened the door and showed Nic the mass destruction known as Ash's room.

Clothes dirty and clean were thrown everywhere, dirty dishes sat scattered about his room, papers and books laid intertwined in the jumbled mess, and a soured mildew smell was emanating from the cramped confines of Ash's closet making Nic feel a little ill.

Nic covered his nose and marveled at the mess. "Someone sleeps in here?"

"Yep," Shima smiled. "This is your master's room. Have fun." She waved and walked down the hall, leaving Nic alone with the mess.

Nic looked around the room; he had no idea where to even begin, the floor was not even visible. Nic picked up some t-shirts off the floor and looked around at the chaos, seeing how little he had done compared to the majority of the disarray.

Was this it? Was this going to be his life for all eternity? Cleaning up and serving a wizard? If someone told Nic all of this yesterday, he would have told them they were on drugs or something. But now, Nic just wanted his old life back.

Nic pushed the thought aside and started collecting the dirty laundry.

#####

Ash walked into his room and stopped. He looked around, amazed. "Wow."

Nic stood by his master's bed, folding Ash's laundry that he took the liberty to clean off the floor and launder. Nic stacked the folded clothes and set them in Ash's dresser, which Nic also took the time to sort and organize. The floor was completely picked up and vacuumed, the bed had fresh new sheets on it and was neatly made, the room was dusted, and the room furniture was polished which left the room smelling like lemon-scented cleaner.

"I-Is this my room?" Ash asked, stepping outside to make sure he was at the correct door and not a different room.

"This better damn well be you room," Nic muttered, still cleaning, "I've been at this for hours." Nic shot Ash a look of annoyance.

Ash whistled. "Dang Nic, you did awesome."

"Thanks," Nic said sarcastically.

"I mean... wow... You can actually see the floor." Ash was in total awe. He had never seen his room so clean before.

"I hope you can after how long I've been in here. You act like you never cleaned your room before." Nic noted, hanging a shirt up in Ash's closet.

Ash was silent for a bit before admitting, "I haven't."

Nic paused what he was doing and looked at Ash. "What?"

"I have never cleaned my room before," Ash repeated.

"How have you never cleaned your room before?" Nic asked, amazed.

"Shima always does it." The wizard shrugged.

Nic finished the laundry and set a hamper by the door. "Well, I'm not doing it again. So if you will please put all dirty clothes in this hamper, you can take them to the laundry room at the end of each week to be cleaned." Nic instructed. "As for dirty dishes, please take them to the kitchen when you are finished because I won't be taking them for you."

"Dully noted," Ash said, "My uncle has a job for you."

Nic sighed. "Wasn't this punishment enough?"

"He would like you to clean the attic," Ash explained.

Nic huffed and muttered, "Apparently not."

"Okay, I'll see you later," Ash said, sitting on his bed and picking up a video game controller.

Nic muttered a few things to himself and walked out, realizing he had no idea where the attic was. He looked around and walked down the halls of the second floor. He came to the banister of the grand stairwell overseeing the living room. Down below, Shima was polishing the coffee table. "Shima, where's the attic?"

Shima looked up and raised an eyebrow. "Why do you need to know?" She asked.

"I have orders to clean the attic," Nic explained to the female familiar.

"Are you finished with Ash's room?" She curiously asked.

"Yes," Nic informed her with a smug smile.

She was surprised, "Very good, you're fast."

"Thanks." Nic accepted the compliment. "Anyway, Ash said I had to clean the attic. Do you know where that is?"

Shima laughed at the question. "Nicky, I know where everything is." She purred and strolled up the stairs to walk with Nic down the hall and up a different flight of stairs.

As they walked, Shima gave a small tour of the house. The house had four stories if you included the attic. The first floor held the basement, the store, living room, kitchen, dining area, and the laundry room. The second floor was comprised of everyone's bedrooms and the study. The third floor held a training room and a few guest bedrooms, which rarely housed guests. The final floor was the attic. As they walked down the hall of the third floor, a rope dangled in the middle of the hallway. Shima gave the rope to Nic. "Pull it down."

Nic pulled rope and the stairs came down, bringing dust along with it. Nic covered his mouth and coughed. He looked up the stairs, seeing how dark it would be up there. "Is there a flashlight I can use?" Nic asked.

Shima laughed heartily. "No need for one. You're a familiar, you can see in the dark." She assured Nic.

Nic gave her a doubtful look, but climbed up the stairs, thinking he could attempt to find a light switch first. But as he climbed the steps to the attic and was thrust into the darkness, his eyes shifted as if he was seeing through night vision goggles. Unknowingly to him, his eyes shifted from their normal red to red and black. There were a lot of boxes and plastic covered furniture, and they all had a layer of dust about an inch thick covering them. Nic whistled and coughed as some dust got in his throat.

"Good luck Nicky." Shima called and left Nic to clean once again.

Nic looked around and sighed, there was so much. "It's Nic," He muttered mostly to himself as he rolled up the sleeves of his shirt and got to work.

#####

Ash sat at the dining table with Jacob waiting for dinner to be served.

Shima walked out with a tray holding a handmade chicken pot pie and set the dish before her master.

Jacob looked at the food and thanked Shima, who bowed and stood at her master's side.

Nic was the next one to walk out of the kitchen carrying a tray. On the tray was a bowl of soup which he set before Ash. Ash watched Nic as the familiar set out a glass of water and some crackers to accompany the soup. "You look a bit pale. Are you okay?" Ash asked, observing the familiar.

"I'm dead. Of course, I'm pale." Nic answered.

"No. You are very much alive as a familiar; you just look a bit sick." Ash examined.

Jacob nodded. "I noticed that as well."

"I'm fine," Nic assured the two wizards.

Knowing that Ash was going to get nowhere with Nic on the topic of his health, Ash changed subjects. "How far are you on the attic?"

"It has been dusted, but that room is going to take me forever to finish cleaning," Nic informed Ash.

Ash stirred his soup. "You're very fast. That's more than enough for a day's work."

Nic was confused.

"I'm giving you the rest of the night off, relax and find something to do," Ash explained. "Besides, it looks like you are about to pass out."

Nic was caught off guard by the comment. "I do?" Nic asked.

"Yeah, it's pretty obvious." Ash shrugged and stirred his soup. "What is this exactly?"

"It's broccoli cheese soup," Nic answered.

"It smells good." Ash commented and ate a mouthful.

"Good," Nic smiled, "because it's from a can."

Shima giggled and tried to withhold her laughing fit, covering her mouth with her tray and turning away. Jacob smiled and ate a spoonful of the chicken pot pie Shima hand-made for him.

Ash looked down at his dinner of soup from a can and he could not help but laugh. Once he finished laughing, Ash cleared his throat to try and sound serious. "This is good for tonight, but from now on I would like homemade meals please." Ash requested, trying to be polite to Nic.

As a wizard, Ash had all the power over Nic and could force the familiar to do anything. But as a friend, Ash wanted to be on the same level as Nic and have the familiar know that he is not going to purposefully order Nic around all the time.

Nic nodded, thinking how much of a pain that would be to hand-make everything when opening a can or box was so much easier. "Yeah, I hear you."

"Good." Ash smiled and ate another bite of his dinner.

Nic watched Shima as she stood beside her master throughout dinner; Nic did the same, trying to copy her.

During dinner, the two wizards talked and ate. When they were finished, Shima cleaned up Jacob's dishes and Nic did the same for Ash.

Before leaving, Ash turned to Nic and suggested that once Nic was done with the dishes, he should get some rest.

Nic took the dishes to the kitchen and rolled up his sleeves even higher before washing the dirty dishware.

Shima joined Nic in the sink not long after to wash her own dishes. She looked at Nic and sighed. "You are only a changeling and I have been very harsh with you today. I am sorry. You must be so scared and look at you." Shima dried her hands on a towel and gently touched Nic's face. "Your color is gone and you have a fever. I will take care of your chores. Go to bed." She ordered the young familiar, shooing him out of her kitchen.

Nic did not disagree, he walked out of the kitchen, but stopped short of the doorway. Nic thought and turned around, "But Ash said..."

"Ash is not here," Shima cut Nic off, "And neither should you. Go to bed." Shima ordered.

"Are you sure?" Nic asked.

Shima washed the dishes, smiling. "Go to your room, Nicky."

"But..."

Nic froze as a steak knife stuck into the frame of the doorway, barely an inch from his face. Nic's eyes widened as he looked at the knife and then at Shima.

Shima looked up, never needing to look to know that she hit her mark. She smiled at Nic mischievously. "I said, to go to bed Nicky."

Nic grew rigid. "Yes, ma'am." He obeyed, not wanting to piss her off any more than he already had. Nic walked up the stairs and instead of continuing down the hall to his room, he took the other stairwell up to the third floor.

#####

Nic held a violin he found while cleaning the attic. Nic cared for it, cleaned it, and tried to tune it, being careful to not accidently snap the old strings. Once the violin was properly cared for, Nic took the bow and played a soft tune on the old strings.

#####

After not finding Nic in his room, Ash scoured the house looking for the young familiar. A soft melody tickled his ears and he carefully followed, walking up a flight of stairs which led to the attic. Ash found Nic playing a tune on an old antique violin with worn down strings. Nic finished his melody, and Ash applauded.

Nic jumped, startled by Ash's applause "What are you doing here?"

"I should be asking you the same thing. And why are you in the dark?" Ash asked, only able to see Nic from the moonlight the attic's window let it. "Didn't I tell you to get some bed rest?"

"It was a suggestion, not an order," Nic muttered.

Ash nodded. "I'll remember that. You play very well."

"Thanks," Nic said putting the violin back in its old case. "It's a pretty violin."

"Really?" Ash asked, not seeing much in the old run down instrument or much at all in the dark.

"It's beautiful; the black painted wood, the rose symbols carved into it, everything about its design is beautiful." Nic said, tracing the rose carved designs.

"You really like that silly violin," Ash observed.

"Like you like your silly cards." Nic countered, driving home a point. Nic packed up the violin and put it back where he found it.

Ash watched Nic in the dark, his eyes slowly adjusting, "You can keep it; no one in this household plays instruments."

"I can have it?" Nic asked, surprised.

Ash shrugged. "Why not?"

Nic pulled the violin back out and looked at it again, this time from an owner's perspective. "Thank you." Nic smiled, "With some new strings and a polishing, she'll be as good as new."

Ash smiled, finally seeing Nic happy about something today. "We can go to the music store after school Monday and pick some supplies up, but for now, let's get you in bed."

Nic picked up the violin and followed his master to his bedroom.

Ash escorted Nic to his bedroom, "Shima has probably said this, but all the clothes in your room were picked out specifically for you and are the correct size. Feel free to use whatever you want."

Nic nodded. "Thanks."

"My room is just next door, if you have any problems, please come to me," Ash advised Nic. "I will leave you alone, good night." Ash offered Nic a smile and walked down the hall to his room.

"Good night." Nic returned the sentiment as Ash walked to his room. Nic walked into his bedroom and closed the door behind him, locking it. He leaned against the door and sighed, today had been a long day.

Nic leaned his new violin against the wall and yawned as he looked around his room. Nic scrounged through the dresser and found some pajama bottoms to wear. He walked into his personal bathroom and figured out how to turn the shower on.

After successfully getting the hot water going, Nic stripped down and got in. As the hot water rolled down his body as he showered, Nic relaxed and tried to get as much anxiety out of his mind as he could. Nic washed his hair, trying to see if someone dyed his hair black as some type of horrible prank or if this was really happening. Nic monitored the water to see if it turned black, but nothing happened. Nic finished his shower and dried off before dressing in his black pajama bottoms. Nic turned the lights out to his room and his eyes shifted subconsciously as they did in the attic. His red irises glowed as the black took over the white of his eyes, allowing him to be able to see perfectly in the complete darkness. Nic walked over to the bed and curled up under the covers. In the pitch darkness, Nic watched the ceiling fan spin. He watched the fan spin and spin, his eyes slowly grew heavy and he fell asleep.

Jacob knocked on Ash's bedroom door at midnight.

Ash answered the door, still awake and playing video games.

"Your familiar needs to be fed and I'm going to make sure he's feeding properly," Jacob said.

Ash nodded and stepped out into the hall. Ash quietly closed the door behind him as he followed his uncle a little down the hall to Nic's room.

Jacob was not just a wizard, he was a witch doctor. Jacob's clients were typically other witches, wizards, and sometimes familiars; if something was wrong, they came to Jacob. Ash loved his Uncle's line of work and studied magic hard to be just like him.

Ash quietly tried to open the door, but Nic's room was locked.

Jacob dug in his pocket and pulled out a ring of keys, picking through them. "I figured he would try to lock us out," He whispered and quietly unlocked the door.

The two opened the door to see the sleeping familiar inside. Ash looked at his Uncle. "What do we do?"

"We are going to test his instincts," Jacob explained. "Give me your hand."

Ash obeyed, giving Jacob his hand.

Jacob pulled out a dagger from his pocket, the same one Ash used to make Nic's familiar body and unsheathed it. "Sorry about this." He apologized in advance and dug the sharp tip into Ash's fingertip.

Ash watched as blood pooled at the prick and rolled down his finger. Ash heard a rustle and looked up.

In the darkness, Ash could see a set of red eyes glowing.

"His sense of smell is superb," Jacob muttered, watching the glowing eyes. "A familiar is never conscious completely when they are feeding, they become animals driven by hunger." Jacob educated Ash as the glowing eyes slowly approached them, like an animal stalking its prey.

Nic slinked over and hissed at Jacob, baring his fangs.

"What's going on?" Ash asked Jacob, startled at Nic's reaction to his Uncle.

"Nic is not Nic right now. He's just an animal and this animal is telling me that I am way too close to his food source." Jacob explained and raised his arms in surrender to back away from Ash.

Once Jacob was a safe enough distance from Ash, Nic approached Ash to smell him. Nic found the source of the blood and licked up the few drops to heal the wound.

"Thanks," Ash said before Nic grabbed Ash's arm with force, smelling him. Ash looked at his uncle. "What's he doing now?"

"He's hungry. That was only a taste tease for him." Jacob informed. "He's looking for a proper place to feed."

Nic used his other arm and held Ash around the waist as he smelled the wizard.

"This is weird," Ash whispered, not liking how Nic was holding him still.

Nis smelled along Ash's arm, leading all the way to Ash's shoulder and neck. Nic stopped along a spot on the crook of Ash's neck and sniffed the spot fixedly.

Ash looked at his uncle, this was beyond weird.

Nic smelled the spot and began to lick Ash's neck.

Ash gasped, it tickled and he shied away from Nic for a second.

Nic hissed and held onto Ash tighter, holding him still as he licked the spot on Ash's neck. Nic's tongue prodded the skin, looking for a thick vein to sink his fangs into. Nic targeted a vein and bit Ash, sinking his fangs deep into the flesh of the wizard's neck.

Ash winced at the bite mark and tried to relax as Nic drank.

The familiar was awkward at first, drinking messily and getting blood all over his face and on Ash's clothes. Eventually, Nic figured out how to drink in time with Ash's heartbeats, making the process a lot less messy. The familiar drank, drawing out more blood than he had earlier that morning.

Once Nic was finished drinking, he cleaned up the wound licking it clean to not waste a single drop of blood and proceeded to clean his face of blood as well. No longer interested with Ash, Nic returned to bed and fell back to sleep.

Jacob smiled. "Easy enough. His instincts are spot on."

Ash nodded and rubbed his neck, he could still feel where Nic's fangs punctured his skin and the pressure of the pull of his blood through his veins as Nic drank.

Jacob motioned for Ash to follow him out. Jacob closed the door and locked the room back up, "Let's get some sleep. Today has been a long day."

Ash agreed to that and they walked down the hallway.

Chapter 7

Shima was up at the crack of dawn to begin cooking breakfast for Jacob. She walked to Nic's room to wake the young familiar up but stopped when she found Nic's door locked. She sighed and walked through the door as if it was not even there. It was another special skill familiars could perform, the ability to choose what to touch is very useful on a daily basis when familiar could not be seen by humans.

Nic was still sleeping, snuggled under the warm sheets.

Shima pulled up her skirt, attached her thigh was a whip, her familiar weapon. She unraveled it and whirled it around once before snapping it in Nic's tiny, empty room.

Nic sat up startled. "What the…?" He gasped and rubbed his sleepy, red eyes.

"I ought to pop you one time with this." She hissed, coiling the whip back up. "A familiar never locks out their master." She scolded.

"I'm not a familiar," Nic muttered, running a hand through his bedhead. He looked at his door, seeing it still locked. "Wait, how did you get in?"

"Familiars can touch whatever they want at will, which includes doors." Shima educated before getting down to business. "Now you are going to put on your dress clothes, vest, and tie; tame that horrendous bedhead of yours and come make your master some breakfast."

"And if I don't?" Nic challenged.

Shima smiled maliciously. "So help me Nic, I will tie you up with this and drag you to the kitchen." She waved her whip threateningly before strapping it back to her leg.

"I'm up." Nic yawned with a sigh.

Shima walked out of the bedroom. "Meet me in the kitchen," She called to Nic from down the hall.

Nic yawned again and got out of bed. He felt much better than he did yesterday. Nic was energized and strong, ready to run marathons; oddly enough, he was full yet he had not eaten in a day or so. Nic shrugged it off, thinking it was a perk of being a familiar. He dressed in his uniform of dress clothes and brushed his hair before going to the kitchen like Shima directed.

Nic walked in as Shima poured some pancake batter into a skillet. Getting the idea, he began to prepare breakfast for Ash. Nic collect some supplies from around the kitchen. "Shima, can I ask you a few things?"

"Sure Nicky." She smiled and flipped a pancake.

Nic looked at her annoyed. "First, can you please stop calling me that?"

"Okeydokey, Nicky boy." She giggled, thinking how fun it was to tease the young familiar.

Nic sighed and returned to his task. "How does Ash take his eggs?"

"Sunnyside up over rice."

"Rice, okay," Nic muttered to himself as he searched the kitchen for some rice.

Shima smiled. "As much as I love your enthusiasm, you may take your sweet time Nicky. It's Sunday. Ash won't be waking for another hour or two. I mostly woke you so you can begin cleaning."

Nic slowed down, looking at the ingredients he had collected.

Shima glanced over at Nic's ingredients and frowned. "What are you going to make?" She asked, examining his choice of ingredients.

"I'm going to fry that egg and make some sausage for accompaniment."

"Good plan," Shima smiled, "But one slight hiccup."

Nic looked over at Shima with an eyebrow raised.

"Your master is a vegetarian," Shima informed Nic.

"Oh..." Nic quickly put the sausage back into the refrigerator.

Shima returned to cooking her pancakes. "Ash always enjoys fresh fruit salad and coffee." Shima hinted, trying to help out the young familiar.

Nic set up the rice to begin cooking and collected some fruit from the refrigerator to cut up for a fruit salad.

Jacob walked in, yawning. "Morning Nic. How are my two favorite familiars?"

"Morning Mr. Jacob." Nic greeted, watching Jacob enter the kitchen.

Shima chuckled. "We are faring fine, and making our masters a breakfast of champions." She smiled.

Jacob kissed Shima, "So pancakes with wiped cream?"

"If that is what you wish?" Shima whispered against Jacob's lips.

Nic looked away, a little embarrassed. Wait, were Shima and Jacob a thing? Nic pushed the thought aside and continued working on Ash's breakfast.

#####

Ten o'clock was more than enough time to sleep in, Nic thought as he walked down the hall with a tray of Ash's breakfast. Nic stopped at the wizard's door and knocked. "Ash, I have breakfast for you. I thought you would want to eat in bed."

No response came from Ash's room. "I'm coming in," Nic warned, barging in.

Ash was still sleeping, buried underneath a pile of blankets in the dark room. Nic sighed and set the tray down on Ash's desk. He shook Ash's shoulder gently. "Ash..." Nic said softly.

Ash moved a little bit, groaning.

"Ash..."Nic repeated, getting a little louder.

"What do you want?" Ash mumbled, rubbing his eyes.

"I have your breakfast and it's getting cold."

Ash rubbed his eyes and sat up a little in bed, "Breakfast in bed?"

"Yep." Nic picked up the silver tray.

Ash smoothed down the sheets and grabbed a hair tie off his nightstand to pony up his bedhead. As usual, when ponying up his hair, Ash's bangs fell out and framed his face.

Nic carefully set the tray in Ash's lap as Ash examined the spread. A nice hot cup of black coffee with steam rising off it sat in the right corner, compared to the left corner where a cool refreshing bowl of fruit salad sat containing a jumbled assortment of oranges slices, grapes, blueberries, banana slices, sliced strawberries, and apple slices. The main course was a bowl of rice with a single egg over the top with a bright yellow yoke. "This looks really good." Ash complimented Nic.

Nic nodded, "Thanks, Shima told me your favorite stuff so I just went from there."

Ash gently took a spoon and popped the yoke, letting its contents bleed over the rice underneath it.

Nic pulled out Ash's rollie-desk chair and sat in it. "Shima also told me you're a vegetarian," Nic said, trying to keep conversation.

Ash ate a bite of the egg with rice, it was really good. "I am, eating meats and stuff gets me sick. I think it's the hormones or something. This is really good by the way, you're an amazing cook."

"Thanks." Nic smiled and thought for a bit. "Can I ask you a few things?"

"Go for it," Ash said around a mouthful of fruit salad. "Just don't make the questions too difficult, I just woke up." He joked.

Nic laughed softly. "So, I was cooking this morning with Shima and your Uncle came in. Are Shima and Mr. Jacob, a thing?" He curiously asked.

Ash almost choked on his fruit salad from laughing.

Nic watched with wide eyes, ready to perform a Heimlech if need arisen.

Ash eventually took control over his choking fit and cleared his throat with some coffee. "Okay. I will explain, just don't get freaked out."

"I promise," Nic said, a little nervous to hear what Ash was about to tell him.

"The answer is yes," Ash said, answering the question before he explained. "You see, when a familiar is made, the blood of the witch or wizard draws a soul that is most similar to them to the familiar's body. With my Uncle it was Shima's soul, with me it was your soul. Anyway, the soul bound to the familiar's body is the perfect complement to the witch or wizard's soul. There are many things you can call it kindred spirits, soul mates, but basically, it means that the souls are very compatible. The bond formed between the servant and master is so strong, they can push their bond further and become lovers, which is what my Uncle and Shima have done."

"So, they're soul mates?" Nic asked, trying to keep up.

"Yes and no. There is no such thing as soul mates, only compatible souls." Ash explained. "Soul mate is a word humans made up to make themselves sound romantic. In the world there are billions of souls, sometimes there are hundreds at a given time that are just as compatible with your soul. You never realize how many souls are compatible with yours because of language barriers, location, distance, age differences, gender, and so on." Ash explained.

"Is it common for witches and wizards to form romantic attachments to their familiars?" Nic asked.

"That is another yes and no answer. It depends on both parties, just like any other relationship." Ash explained.

Nic nodded. He was pretty sure that he understood.

"To me, my relationship with you is strictly master and servant. Yet I also see you as a companion and friend. You're like a best friend to me." Ash smiled. "I've known you ever since we were little. We were best friends back in kindergarten."

Nic remembered that, "Yeah that was before Trisha moved to Amington."

The two were silent for a second until Ash broke the silence with a small laugh.

"Remember that one time in first grade when you stole my juice box?" Ash smiled, remembering.

"That was after you stole my fruit snack!" Nic countered, defending himself.

Ash laughed, "You're right. Well... I never really had a friend before." Ash admitted.

Nic nodded looked down at the wheels of the rolly chair. "You were always the kid playing with cards in the back of the classroom."

"Yeah... well, you remember, I was never good at talking to people." Ash sighed, "No matter how much I wanted to, people always seemed bored with me. I had no one I could talk to after we stopped being friends."

Nic remembered Ash. "We use to always be together." Nic laughed a little thinking, "We use to play tag and you always cried."

"I did not!" Ash defended. "You always pushed me down when you tagged me!"

"I remember!" Nic laughed, "The teacher use to get on to both of us because you would tackle me after I pushed you down and we would fight. We beat the snot out of each other as kids."

"Then we would be mad at each other as the teacher put us in time out. But the second we were out we would do the same thing over again." Ash smiled, thinking back.

"I had forgotten all about that," Nic admitted.

"Yeah… well, you kind of forgot about me." Ash mentioned, sighing softly. "Trisha moved to Amington when we were in first grade. You slowly stopped playing with me and started playing with her. When second grade rolled around, I never really saw you anymore."

Nic nodded, looking back down at the wheels of the rolly chair. "I'm sorry Ash."

"The older I got the more my powers fluctuated. I had difficulty keeping them under wraps and so I became more reclusive. I only talked to a few people, but none of them were as fun to talk to as you were. You were really smart and got into the gifted courses and you spent all of your free time with Trisha, I never really got an opportunity to talk to you again. I have to admit, though, I have enjoyed your company the last two days." Ash confessed.

"Thanks, Ash." Nic smiled and pushed a lock of black hair behind his ear. "Can I ask for a favor?"

"What is it?" Ash asked before sipping his coffee.

"I want to see my family." Nic requested.

"Nic, we need to be careful," Ash warned his familiar.

"Please Ash, they're my family. I have to see how they're doing."

"No." Ash decided.

"Please? I have to make sure that Cassie is okay." Nic begged.

"Cassie?" Ash asked.

"My baby sister," Nic said softly.

"You have a baby sister?"

Nic nodded. "She's five years old."

"What about your brother? I think his name was Zachary, wasn't it?" Ash paused to think.

Ash remembered Nic's parents, Mr. and Mrs. Russell. Nic was the youngest son and had an old brother named Zachary who was eight years older than him. Ash remembered going to the park with Nic and Zac tagging along to babysit.

Nic's hands clenched and unclenched. "You don't know," Nic said softly. "We stopped being friends long before that," He muttered to himself.

"Long before what?" Ash asked, eating a spoonful of rice and egg, oblivious.

"Zachary died a long time ago."

"W-What?!" Ash asked shocked, almost dropping his spoon.

"I was thirteen when it happened," Nic said, remembering. "Zachary was attending college at Tempton University. It was Thanksgiving and Zac was supposed to come home for the family dinner, but he never came. We called his cell phone and his roommate's cellphone, but we could never reach him and his roommate had no idea where he was. Police called us the next morning and told us that they found Zac's car at the bottom of a ditch. Apparently, he had lost control and hit the guardrail too hard causing his car to flip over the edge. At the time, Cassie was only a baby so she doesn't remember and never will. But the grief my parents had quickly turned into arguing. My father tried to drink the problems away and my mom suffered from depression. The arguing got so bad some nights; I sometimes would run away and go to Trisha's house. About a year later, my parents split up. They never got a divorce because they still loved each other, but the pain of losing Zac was unbearable to them. So, they stopped living together and blamed themselves for what happened." Nic explained.

"I'm so sorry Nic. I didn't know." Ash said softly.

Nic shrugged it off. "You wouldn't know. It happened a long time ago and we weren't exactly friends then."

"I know, but still... I remember Zachary, he was an awesome guy. I use to be jealous of you because I am an only child, I wanted a brother so bad. Zac played soccer with us, tag, and he even tried to scare us when we were telling ghost stories during the sleepovers at your house. He was really cool."

"Yeah, but he died several years ago, and it really did a number on my family. I just want to make sure everyone is okay and that my death doesn't have the same effect, or worse."

Ash nodded. "Let me finish breakfast and we'll go to your house after that. Deal?"

Nic was surprised that Ash agreed. He smiled, "Deal."

Chapter 8

Ash drove to Nic's house, which was approximately ten minutes away by car, and pulled into a suburb. Nic's house was the second on the end, a typical tan two-story cookie-cutter house. Ash parked his car in front of Nic's house and looked at the familiar. "Are you sure about this?"

Nic nodded. "I just want to check and see that everyone is okay."

Ash sighed and got out of his car.

Nic remembered what Shima said about not having to touch material objects. Nic focused and got out of the car without opening the door, passing through it. Nic's eyes widened and he looked at Ash.

Ash smiled. "Good job."

"How did I do that?" Nic muttered.

Ash laughed and walked up the sidewalk to Nic's house. Ash remembered sleepovers in that house, telling ghost stories, and playing tic-tac-toe on the sidewalk with pavement chalk. Ash walked up the steps of the porch and rang the doorbell. "I won't be able to keep conversation too long," Ash warned Nic, who was following right behind him.

"I just want to look around," Nic assured Ash.

It took a minute, but Nic's mother answered the door. She was a beautiful woman with shoulder length golden blonde hair like Nic use to have. Her eyes were ice blue but were currently red and puffy. It was obvious the woman had been crying recently. She wore a black dress and tried to smile at Ash. "Hello," She said, her voice a bit hoarse. "Are you one of Nic's friends?"

Ash glanced at Nic for a second and nodded solemnly. "I am, Mrs. Russell. You probably don't remember me, but my name is Ash Starnes. I was best friends with Nic when we were little."

Mrs. Russell's eyes widened and she nodded. "I remember you. You and Nic were so close." She turned away from the door and grabbed a tissue to dab her eyes. "Please come in. Sit down and I'll bring us something to drink."

Nic came in with Ash, who of course was not able to be seen by humans, even his parents. "Please don't go through the trouble, Mrs. Russell. I just wanted to see how you were and if there was anything I can do to help."

Mrs. Russell came in with a pitcher of lemonade and two glasses. She set the two glasses on the coffee table and poured some lemonade. "Thank you so much dear, but we're fine. There are plenty of neighbors in our community who are looking out for us. Please sit down. I haven't seen you in forever, let's catch up." She smiled sadly and offered Ash a cup of lemonade.

"Thanks." Ash accepted the cup and sat down on the tan couch as Nic remained standing beside him.

"The last time I saw you, you were still toddling about. My how you've grown up," She looked at Ash in wonder, "You've become quite handsome, are you pretty popular with the ladies?" She grinned.

Ash could see right through Mrs. Russell, she was only trying to get her mind off the recent loss of her son with casual small talk.

Ash laughed softly. "I wish. I'm lucky if a girl looks at me when I hold a door open for her."

Mrs. Russell laughed. "You'll find yourself a perfect someone eventually. How is high school? Are you keeping up with your classes?"

While Nic's mother and Ash talked, Nic looked around his house for the last time. He walked over to the hall where several family photos were hung. He paused in front of the only family photo that the Russells' had all together.

Zac and Nic stood in front of their parents while Nic's mother held a baby Cassie. All the boys wore sky blue dress shirts with black slacks and the two girls wore sky blue dresses for a beautiful family photo.

Ash glanced at Nic looking at the picture. "I'm trying to keep up with my studies. The only class I'm struggling with is pre-calculus."

Mrs. Russell was silent for a bit. "Nic had that class."

Ash nodded. "Nic and I were in the same class, he sat right in front of me actually."

A man walked into the living room where Mrs. Russell and Ash were sitting on the couch. The man had brown hair combed over to the side with a matching brown mustache. He had a bit of a beer gut but it was hidden by his professional dress clothes of khaki slacks and a black dress shirt. His most distinguishing feature was his emerald green eyes.

Ash stood and offered his hand to shake with Mr. Russell. He remembered Mr. Russell taking Ash to the park to play baseball with Nic and Zac.

Mr. Russell smiled and brushed the handshake aside to hug Ash. "You've grown big Ash."

Ash chuckled, "Puberty does that to people."

Mr. and Mrs. Russell laughed; Ash could tell that those two really needed that laugh after all that has happened.

"Sit down. Make yourself comfortable." Mr. Russell suggested. "Tell us, what are you doing after high school?" Mr. Russell sat down beside his wife as Ash sat across from them on a different couch.

"I plan to attend Tempton University to continue my education." Ash lied, giving his generic answer. Not many people responded well to Ash informing them that he was going to become a witch doctor.

"What are you studying?" Mrs. Russell smiled.

"Pharmaceuticals and health," Ash answered, his lie not too far from the truth.

"That's a good field of study." Mr. Russell encouraged.

Ash glanced at Nic and noticed him looking upstairs. "I'm not meaning to be insensitive, but I previously lent Nic a standardized test study book before his passing and I sort of need it. I was wondering if I may go up to his room and look for it?"

"Of course dear, do you know where Nic's room is?" Mrs. Russell asked.

"It's still upstairs, right? Last door on the left?" Ash asked, making sure.

"Yes, if you need any help looking, please don't hesitate to ask." Mrs. Russell smiled. "Take as long as you need."

"Thank you, Mrs. Russell," Ash said, and stood. He walked upstairs, following Nic. Ash watched Nic walked down the hall to his room and stop at a door.

Nic looked at Ash then back at the door, walking through it.

Ash followed right behind him and opened the door at the end of the hall.

Nic was already looking around his room.

Ash closed the door behind him as he watched his familiar.

"I couldn't take it anymore. They were so sad." Nic said, playing with a Newton's cradle on his bookshelf.

"That's because they just lost their son, any parent would be grief stricken." Ash answered and looked around Nic's tidy room.

"I don't want them to be sad," Nic whispered.

"That's not something you have influence over." Ash said and picked up a book off Nic's bookshelf. "Okay, you have three minutes," Ash informed Nic. Ash chose a standardized test booklet and grabbed a pen to write on the front page, 'Property of Ash Starnes'.

"Three minutes?" Nic asked.

Ash nodded. "Any mementos you cannot live without. A picture or something special, give it to me now so I can sneak it out." Ash said and watched Nic search his room. Nic gave Ash a few things such as a few photos of his family and Trisha, a drawing from his baby sister, and a few trinkets from Zac such as a guitar pick and a necklace. Nic eventually stopped wandering about his room and stood confidently with his few choices. "This all?" Ash asked to make sure the handful of items were all Nic wanted.

Nic nodded. "Yeah."

"Alright, let's go," Ash said, stuffing the keepsakes into his pocket and walked out of Nic's room. Ash did not see Nic's parents in the living room as he descended the stairs. Not wanting to leave without saying goodbye, Ash wandered into the kitchen.

Mrs. Russell was making a peanut butter and jelly sandwich for Cassie who sat at the dining table drawing on a piece of paper with a crayon.

Nic walked over to his baby sister and kneeled down beside her. "Hey Cassie," Nic said softly, but he knew that she could not hear him or see him. "I love you." He smiled sadly.

Ash watched for a second as Nic kissed her forehead, but Cassie did not sense a thing.

Cassie had just turned five not too long ago. She had long platinum blonde hair, which Nic predicted would darken with time like his own hair did. She had ice blue eyes just like her mother, but the eyes that use to twinkle with happiness were now dark with depression.

Mrs. Russell cut the crusts off the sandwich and gave it to Cassie before kissing her daughter's forehead.

Ash cleared his throat to make his presence known to Mrs. Russell. "I found my book. Thank you for letting me get it."

"No problem dear. Thank you for coming." Mrs. Russell said, she cleaned her hands and hugged Ash. "Are you coming to the funeral?"

"Yes. I wouldn't miss it. When is it exactly?" Ash asked.

"It's at noon on Tuesday." Mrs. Russell answered.

"I'll definitely be there. Thank you, Mrs. Russell."

"No, thank you, Ash, for coming. I've been wanting to see you for a while," She kissed Ash's cheek. "Feel free to come by anytime." She smiled sadly.

"Of course Mrs. Russell," Ash said. He looked at Cassie and waved. "Bye Cassie."

Cassie did not say anything to the stranger, she only waved bye.

Ash walked out the front door to head to his car with the familiar walking beside him. Ash glanced to his side at Nic, "You okay?" Ash asked as the two were getting into the car.

Nic sat in the passenger seat and looked at his house, before turning to look back at Ash. "I-I want to go home."

"This is your home," Ash answered as he started his car.

"Not anymore." Nic sighed and returned to looking out the window.

Ash smiled sadly. "Let's go home then." Ash put his car into drive and gently pulled away from the Russell house.

Nic watched as his house grew smaller and smaller before finally disappearing behind other houses.

Chapter 9

Ash parked his car in the driveway of the decrepit manor at 666 Livian street. "You need some cheering up and I have some multiplayer video games that have never been played before." Ash planned, getting out of his car.

Nic smiled sadly and phased through the door again to exit the car. "I think I can do that." Nic thought aloud.

"Good, you are off for the day. I don't want you doing chores, making dinner, or serving me in any way. I order you to be your normal self, like when we were kids." Ash ordered.

Nic's red eyes became black as the white of his eyes were consumed by the color.

Ash grinned, seeing Nic's eyes turn colors at the order. "Awesome. Now let's go have some fun!" Ash cheered, leading Nic inside after his eyes returned to their normal color.

#####

Nic held a controller, sitting in Ash's rolly chair as Ash laid on his bed, hanging upside down off the edge as they played a sniper game. Nic glanced over at Ash, then back at the screen to not lose focus. "Do you always play video games upside down?"

"Not always, but it helps me focus," Ash replied, not looking away from the screen.

Nic's character snuck up behind Ash's character and shot him, killing his character.

Ash gasped, shocked, as Nic laughed.

"You don't seem focused to me." Nic laughed.

"Payback is a bitch," Ash warned as his character respawned and resumed looking for Nic's avatar.

Jacob knocked on the door and entered Ash's room.

Nic quickly paused the game, not wanting to lose their place and his winning status.

"Ash, I want you to take over the shop today as I run into town. Shima says that we're running low on groceries." Jacob said, asking his nephew for a favor.

Ash nodded and got up, turning off the game station. "This is a good chance for me to show Nic around."

Nic put the rolly chair back and stood at attention.

"I entrust the shop to you for the next few hours," Jacob said. "I highly doubt we'll be very busy, but if a customer does come in, see to them."

"Nic and I can handle it," Ash assured Jacob.

Nic had no idea what was going on, but he nodded anyway.

Jacob and Ash walked downstairs with Nic following not too far behind.

Shima was holding the front door open, waiting for her master to come.

"Have fun boys." Jacob waved and walked out, Shima following right behind him.

Ash looked at Nic. "When I graduate Amington High, I want to open my own practice."

"What type of practice?" Nic asked, interested.

"A health practice, I want to be a witch doctor," Ash answered like everyone was supposed to know what that meant.

Nic only looked at the wizard confused.

"Come here and look at this." Ash waved Nic over to the door to the right of the fireplace. Nic wondered about that door but never asked anyone. Ash opened the door and stepped aside for Nic to enter.

Inside was a huge room, decorated with beautiful greens, purples, and silvers. Racks of vials and bottles filled with potions lined the walls. In the middle of the room was a comfy green and purple couch with a silver table in front of it. On the table was a crystal ball, a pack of tarot cards, and a book of spells and exorcisms. On the opposite side of the table was a green and purple arm chair matching the couch's color coordination. The room had other things too, such as a bookshelf that was as tall as the ceiling and stretched along the whole wall. It was filled with books about magic, fortune telling, symbolism, and interpretations.

Ash smiled as Nic looked around amazed. "Pretty cool, huh?"

"It is." Nic agreed looking at the different labels on the potion vials.

"After I graduate, I want my own shop like this; I will have to get certified through the Witch and Wizards Health Association, but I believe I can do it once I finish high school."

"This is pretty cool," Nic admitted, still looking around.

"Once I graduate, I plan to attend a magic health college. You and I will have to get certified to run such a business. And, from what I've been told, it's challenging. But

Shima and my Uncle passed and became certified. If they can do it, I believe we can do it too."

Nic was still amazed by the room as he looked around.

"Hey. I made you something yesterday when I was studying with Uncle Jacob." Ash walked over to a chest of drawers and pulled out a box. "I want to see if it works."

Nic walked over and glanced over Ash's shoulder, curious.

Ash pulled out a brown box and opened it. Inside was a black leather cord necklace with a red teardrop stone charm on the end.

"What is that?" Nic asked.

"It's enchanted so it will transform when you do." Ash handed Nic the necklace, smiling.

"Transform? Transform into what?" Nic accepted the necklace and looked it over. The necklace appeared normal, but he did not know if there was some kind of enchantment placed on it.

Ash thought of the perfect way to put the explanation into words. "You know how on Halloween you always see pictures of green witches with warts riding a broomstick with a cat on the end, right?"

Nic nodded. "Yeah."

"Well, the cat is supposed to represent familiars."

"Are you saying that I can turn into a cat?" Nic snorted in disbelief.

"I don't know what you turn into," Ash answered, truthfully. "Familiars are just like people, they are all different, and their forms vary. Shima, like the stereotypical familiar, can actually turn into a black cat."

"So I can turn into an animal?" Nic asked, still doubtful about the extent of his new powers.

Ash nodded and smiled. "That is why I made you this. This necklace is enchanted to turn into a collar when you shift."

Nic looked at the necklace in his hand.

"I want to see it in action and make sure I didn't screw my spells up." Ash clarified.

"I don't know how." Nic sighed, "I didn't even know I can turn into an animal until a few seconds ago."

"It's supposed to be easy, like phasing through doors which you already conquered without any guidance. All you have to do is focus." Ash leaned against the table with the crystal ball.

"But why exactly do I need a collar?" Nic asked.

"In your animal form, people can see you. Reason number one of why you need a collar," Ash began to make a list on his fingers, "So the pound doesn't pick you up off the street like a common stray. Reason number two is if you get lost or somebody finds you, they can contact me. Reason number three, I mark you as my familiar so other witches and wizards know who you belong to if something ever happens. It's like the equivalent of a driver's license in the magical world." Ash explained. "Now put it on already. I want to see your animal form." Ash said getting anxious, he really wanted to know what Nic's animal form was.

Nic sucked it up, knowing that he was not going to win any argument with Ash. He slipped the necklace over his head and admired it momentarily. It was nice. He was not much for necklaces, but it is so lightweight that he barely recognized it was there at all.

    Nic returned his attention to shifting into an animal and focused. He imagined himself becoming an animal, but the harder he focused, the more he realized how stupid he probably looked. Nic opened his eyes.

    Ash watched Nic intently, "When are you going to start shifting?"

    Nic huffed, "I'm working on it. This is harder than it looks, I don't think I can do it."

    "Honestly, it doesn't look easy at all. But," Ash scratched his chin as he thought, "Just think of the first animal that comes to your mind and focus on it. Maybe that will help."

    Nic nodded, that sounded like a workable plan. Nic closed his eyes and focused on his favorite type of animal, a dog. He loved dogs, but he never had one because his mother was allergic to them. As he focused on dogs, his body began to shift and contort.

    Ash watched as Nic became a black dog. Ash was not entirely certain what exactly Nic was. He looked like a wolf, yet he had resemblances of a black Siberian husky.

    Nic panted from his transformation and shook off, fluffing up his fur coat; it took a lot of energy to shift.

    Ash laughed. "I always wanted a dog. No wonder you and Shima don't get along all the time." Ash smiled and kneeled down to pet Nic and examine the collar. The black leather cord enlarged and became a black leather collar around Nic's neck and the red stone became red dog tags which read Nic's name and Ash's address. "Too tight?" Ash asked Nic as he situated the collar.

Nic shook his head no.

"You're not the only familiar in the world who wears a collar, Shima wears one too," Ash informed Nic.

Nic remembered seeing Shima always wear a necklace. The necklace was always the same, a silver bell connected to a different color ribbon; today it was a purple ribbon.

"Okay. All-,"Ash was interrupted by the doorbell. He looked at the door, seeing someone he did not recognize through the glass window. "That's a customer."

Nic looked in the direction of the door with his ears perked up.

"This is the perfect opportunity for you to try out your animal form," Ash instructed Nic.

Nic looked up at Ash confused.

"Just try to get the customer to pet you. It will give you ample proof that other people can see you in this form." Ash gave Nic his mission as they walked to the front door to answer it.

Nic did not know how to walk on four legs and tripped over his paws as he made his way to the door. He quickly got the hang of it and sat down by the grand staircase and watched Ash open the door.

Ash greeted a woman with sun-tanned skin and bleach blonde hair. The wizard invited her inside and led her into the shop.

Nic followed like a shadow, sitting by the couch.

The woman sat down on the couch and gently pet Nic's head, scratching him behind his ears.

Nic felt like melting, the ear scratch felt so good. Something was hitting against Nic's leg and he whipped his head around to look at his tail wagging.

Ash sat in the armchair across the table, smiling at Nic's triumph of human contact. "Hello, what can I do for you today?" He asked politely, getting down to business.

"Is Mr. Starnes not in?" The woman asked.

"I'm afraid not, but I'm Jacob's adopted son. He has taught me everything he knows and I would be more than able to perform what you need." Ash offered his services.

As the two talked about what type of service the woman wanted, Nic slipped out of the store room. He focused, having difficulties as he did before from shifting to his animal form. Nic focused all his desires on becoming human and felt his body shift. Nic's body contorted and shifted back into his human form under those focused desires. Nic looked at his body in amazement, scanning over himself to make sure everything was back to normal with no extra appendages. He quickly got over himself and returned to Ash's side as the woman agreed on getting a tarot card reading for today.

Ash noticed Nic come in, but did not look up to acknowledge him.

Ash shuffled the tarot cards. "Any specific thing you want to talk about today?"

"Well, I've been dating this guy for a year and a half now and I think he's going to propose tonight. But, I'm just not sure if I'm ready to get married." The woman admitted.

"I recommend a three card spread problem solver. I have a lot of experience is three card spreads and I'm very comfortable reading you that way." Ash explained as he drew three random cards from the deck and laid them face down. "Each card represents a step in the problem-solving process." Ash explained and flipped over the first card. "This is your situation card, 'Two of Swords'."

The card flipped over showed a blindfolded woman holding two swords, Nic remembered seeing the same card in his reading on Friday before the accident.

"A conflict of heart and mind is represented in this card. Obviously with your love for this guy, you would be experiencing such a conflict. Next is the problem," Ash flipped over a card with a picture of a man sitting among a throne looking very haughty with nine golden cups surrounding him. At the same time, the man appears inviting as if he wants you to come and enjoy his good fortune. "This card is called 'Nine of Cups', it represents material, emotional, and physical well-being. You want to be happy and this guy might be your solution, you're just uncertain." Ash interpreted and turned the final card over. The last card had a man and woman kissing in a pool of water with the sun shining overhead; an angel appears to be guiding their actions. "This card is called 'The Lovers', and they represent a decision that makes your heart happy."

The woman smiled and stood. "Thank you. This has really helped."

"Are you sure you don't want me to do another reading?" Ash asked as the woman dug into her purse.

"No, I don't need to be told more than I already know." The woman smiled happily.

Nic's eyes widened as the woman pulled out a fifty dollar bill and gave it to Ash.

Ash thanked her and walked her out, acting like a gentleman. When she left, he stuck the money in his pocket and grinned at Nic. "I got skills."

Nic was still amazed. "How come you only charge five dollar fortunes at school, if you are making ten times that?"

"It's called supply and demand, I thought you took basic economics." Ash smiled smugly. "If I set the price too high, no one will pay. If I set it too low everyone would want their fortune told, so I had to find a nice middle ground."

"I knew you gave fortunes, but that was really spot-on," Nic observed.

"Witches and wizards act like psychologists, but we don't base out knowledge on guesses and assumptions. Since you know what they say about assumptions," Ash smirked. "We actually know the possible future events through our magic."

"You were really good at that," Nic stated, impressed. "You told her everything she wanted to hear."

Ash shook his head. "You don't understand. I don't just tell people what they want to hear, I tell them what I know will happen. I only speak the truth. I don't know how the future will unravel, but I can foretell pieces of it. Like when I told your fortune," Ash explained, giving a solid example.

Nic remembered and nodded. "It was just as you said," He muttered, remembering.

"Come on." Ash smiled. "I'm hungry." The young wizard wasted no time by leading the way to the kitchen.

Nic followed Ash and watched him rummage through the cabinets, pulling out a bag of veggie chips.

Satisfied with his findings, Ash sat on a barstool at the island in the middle of the kitchen.

As Ash ate some chips, Nic absent-mindedly wet a wash cloth and began to wipe off the counters. "As a familiar, you can do a lot of new stuff," Ash mentioned with a mouthful of chips.

"Like what?" Nic asked, cleaning up.

"Not only can you shift into a dog and walk through things, but you are faster and stronger now," Ash said. "You have advanced healing abilities and extremely high pain tolerance."

Nic laughed, "So am I like Superman or something?"

Ash chuckled, "It's more of an 'or something'."

The two were silent for a second until Nic thought aloud. "Shima said the other day that a familiar's job is to serve their masters."

"Yes?" Ash nodded, knowing that there was more than that on Nic's mind.

"She also said that in exchange for our servitude, the master gives us clothing, shelter, protection, and they feed us."

Ash nodded, eating a mouthful of chips, all of that was true so far. "Is there a question here somewhere?"

"Ash, I haven't eaten since lunchtime on the day I died. That was more than two days ago and I've been perfectly fine," Nic explained.

"Ah, I forgot," Ash muttered around a mouthful of chips like it was no big deal. "Well, you actually have eaten twice since you got here. But you may not remember because you were somewhat unconscious both times."

Nic was confused. "What do you mean by that?"

"Nic, you can't eat normal food anymore." Ash pulled out a chip from his bag and offered it to Nic. "A familiar can't consume human food. Try it."

Nic took the chip Ash offered, it was a normal veggie chip. Nic had many of them before due to his mom's diet. He popped it into his mouth and chewed. The chip scrapped against his taste buds like sandpaper leaving a horrible taste in his mouth like sawdust. Nic ran over to the sink and tried to spit up as much as he could of the chip.

Ash was surprised by Nic's reaction. "You okay?"

"Yeah," Nic coughed, spitting up a few more crumbs. "That was horrible," He muttered.

"The same thing will happen if you eat any type of human food."

"Then what do I eat?" Nic asked, scared.

Ash ate a few more chips and smiled. "Sure you don't want anymore?" He teased, passing the bag over to Nic.

Nic pushed the bag away, looking a little green. His color returned when Ash put them back in the cabinet. "What do I eat?" Nic repeated.

"Familiars eat one thing." Ash stalled, not answering Nic.

"Which is?" Nic asked, hating how Ash was leading him on.

"Blood." Ash ominously said.

Nic's eyes widened. "Wh-what?"

"Relax, you aren't a vampire or anything. Familiars can only drink one type of blood; the blood of their masters." Ash explained.

"I-Just wait, what?" Nic asked, still not fully understanding.

"When created, a witch or wizard bounds the familiar's soul to the new body with their blood. The blood pact is made and the familiar may only partake of the blood given to them in the pact."

"So you made a blood pact with me?" Nic inquired, trying to get the story straight.

"Yes. I gave you my blood and thus you can only drink my blood."

"What happens if I refuse to drink?" Nic asked.

"Nic, don't get any funny ideas," Ash warned. "If you refuse to drink you will get really sick and then I will have to order you to drink. I don't want to demean you like that, but I will if you force me."

The two were silent for a while until Nic spoke up again. "How often do familiars have to drink?"

"You are a young familiar, a changeling," Ash explained. "So you need it daily for the first couple of years. After that, your body will have the say on when it needs to feed. Your body may need it daily, weekly, monthly, heck I have heard rumors of certain familiars having yearly feedings. It's all a matter of bodily need."

"How often does Shima drink?" Nic asked.

"Every day," Ash stated bluntly. "Typically a familiar likes drinking from their masters similarly to how a human likes to eat at a buffet. A human doesn't need a buffet meal every day, but it's a nice luxury."

"I just... that sounds disgusting." Nic admitted.

"It's for your health Nic, think of it like taking vitamins or something."

"I think I can handle being sick."

"No Nic. Come here." Ash ordered, rolling up his sleeve.

Nic's eyes flashed red and turned black as his body forced him to walk over to Ash.

Ash offered his arm to Nic. "You get to choose, right now or tonight when you are unconscious?"

"Ash, please don't make me do this." Nic pleaded.

"I'm giving you the choice Nic, I won't make you do it now. But I prefer you to go ahead and get it over with. You need to have your first conscious feeding session soon." Ash said, rationalizing with Nic.

Nic glared at Ash and knocked his arm aside and stormed out of the room.

Ash watched Nic leave. He knew he had been tough on Nic; but if Nic was not going to drink the easy way, Ash was going to have to do it the hard way.

#####

Ash walked down the hall and stopped at Nic's bedroom door at one in the morning. Ash pulled a safety pin from his pocket and unfastened it. Just like the night before, he dug the pin into the tip of his index finger, drawing blood.

Ash watched the finger bleed and looked up, startled. Somehow in those few seconds, Nic smelled Ash's blood and followed the scent out to Ash. "Hi, Nic."

Nic looked at him with black and red eyes, he took Ash's finger and sucked on it. He pulled some blood out, but quickly found it an insufficient way to drink. Nic healed the wound and looked for a better place to feed.

Nic found a spot on Ash's shoulder and bite down, drawing blood and drinking from the wizard.

"I'm sorry Nic." Ash relaxed in Nic's arms as the familiar drank. "You need to become use to this. If you don't, life will only become harder."

Chapter 10

Shima knocked on Nic's door at six in the morning, waking the young familiar up.

Nic sat up and rubbed his sleepy red eyes.

"Up and at 'em," Shima called through the door. "You need to make Ash breakfast before school," Shima instructed the young familiar before continuing to walk down the hall and leaving Nic to his own devices.

Nic managed to pull himself out of bed and dressed in his uniform. He finished getting ready and walked downstairs to the kitchen where Shima was making breakfast for Jacob. Nic whipped up some batter for blueberry pancakes and poured some into a skillet to begin cooking.

An awkward silence swallowed the kitchen as the two cooked.

After a long silence, Shima could not take it anymore. "Listen, I know you are young and everything, but sulking over a little blood is ridiculous." Shima scolded. "Ash told Jacob and me everything that transpired last night," She informed her charge.

"I'm not upset because of blood," Nic muttered.

"Then what?" Shima asked.

"My humanity," Nic replied vaguely as he started the coffee maker.

"You are not human anymore, so why does that matter?" Shima peeled and began to slice up a banana.

"It matters!" Nic argued getting defensive.

"Okay, fine. What is your definition of humanity, Nicky?" Shima paused chopping up the banana and held her knife with delicate care.

Nic eyed the knife carefully in her hands, knowing her potential of what she could do with it. He backed up from her to the stove where the pancakes were cooking. "Having qualities of a human," Nic answered, unable to think of any other way to define it.

"So, what about being a familiar is so different from being a normal boring human? Is it the blood drinking?" Shima asked.

Nic looked away. He searched through the cabinets, pretending to be looking for syrup, knowing that it was in the pantry. He reached up for a top cabinet door and quickly pulled his hand away as a knife buried itself into the wooden door. "Are you crazy?!" He shouted looking at Shima, who had already pulled another knife from the kitchen drawer and was continuing to cut bananas.

"I already have one angsty teen in this house. I don't need two. I figured that you would have more sense than your knucklehead of a master. You're smarter, older, and excel in more things." Shima explained and set her knife down. She walked over to Nic and leaned over him.

"Wh-what are you doing?" Nic stuttered as Shima pressed her chest against his as she leaned over Nic. Nic's pale complexion darkened with blush.

Shima rolled her eyes. "You are such a virgin." She muttered and turned off the burner of the stove which Nic was using to make pancakes. Shima righted herself, still close to Nic, but not intimately close like she was before.

"Come here," She gently took Nic's hand and led him to the barstools at the island counter. "Sit, let's talk," She said in a soothing voice, for a second, Nic swore that she sounded just like his mother.

Nic shifted in his seat. "There's not much to talk about," Nic muttered, looking away.

"Nicky please talk to me." Shima pleaded softly.

"I'm sorry. But I have nothing to say." Nic said, looking at the counter and tracing some patterns with his finger. His eyes, never meeting hers.

Shima wrapped an arm around Nic's shoulders. "I think it's the opposite. I believe that you have too much to say."

Nic glanced at her, avoiding the eyes, then returned his attention back to tracing designs on the counter.

"When I was your age, as a familiar, I was just like you," Shima said, delving into a story since Nic was not talking and she could not stand any more awkward silences. "Every familiar is alike in the beginning. We are skeptical, scared, and we don't know what to do. When Jacob first told me how I needed to feed, I about clawed his eyes out." Shima informed, making Nic chuckle at the thought of Shima attacking Jacob with her nails. "At first, I thought Jacob was just trying to take advantage of me. But then I realized that witches and wizards do it for our health. Nic, Ash is just looking out for you. He is trying to pay you back for being such a good servant."

Nic paused his finger tracing on the counter a second before continuing.

"You can never return to being human. That part of you has died and this is what rose from the ashes. This is the new you." Shima smiled softly, running a hand through Nic's soft black hair. She gently pulled the teen familiar closer into a warm hug. "You are nothing more than an infant in this new world, but this life is filled with magic and adventure. There are many new things for you to do and experience, things that you have only seen in your wildest dreams." She paused when she felt Nic's shoulders shake slightly. She looked at Nic whose head was hung; tears collected on his nose and fell. "Oh, Nicky." She purred, and lovingly pulled him to her chest. "It's okay to cry." She gently rubbed Nic's back.

"I-I don't want to be a f-familiar," Nic wept against Shima's shoulder, finally cracking. "I-I want to be human a-again. I want to go home to my f-family a-and be with Tr-Trisha."

"I know dear." Shima cooed and rubbed the young familiar's back.

Nic continued to cry against her shoulder.

Shima hummed a soft tune to a lullaby as she gently ran her fingers through Nic's hair and rubbed his back.

Nic quieted down as Shima started to put words to the tune, wanting to hear the lullaby.

"Hush my child, save the tear.
Nothing will harm you when I am near.
Keep all your tears at bay,
So I may kiss the pain away.
Hush my baby, please don't cry
So you can hear this lullaby.

Now we are here, all alone,
Never forget this song's tone.
I love you with all my heart,
So we will never be apart."

When Shima finished her song, Nic wiped his tears away. "That was beautiful, I never heard it before."

"Thanks," She said softly. "I use to sing it for my son all the time."

"Your son?" Nic asked.

Shima smiled. "I don't look old enough to have a child, huh?" She smiled and laughed softly, still holding Nic. "Anthony was only a baby when I died."

Nic was curious now and he sat up a little straighter so he could listen to the story.

Shima smiled and pushed a strand of hair back behind Nic's ear so she could see Nic's red eyes.

"In the 1700's everyone was moving to the big city to get an opportunity to work in the new factories. I wanted to go too, but being a simple girl from the country I had no experience in big cities and the thought somewhat scared me. So, I stayed on the farms." Shima explained, beginning her story.

"Wait, are you telling me that you were present for the industrial revolution?" Nic asked, captivated.

"Yes. I do believe that is what scholars call it now." Shima said thinking. "I married a nice man and we settled down. I then gave birth to a beautiful healthy baby boy and we named him Anthony. My husband left to go to the city to support us, but he never came back." Shima said softly. "I was left alone with Anthony and no way to pay the bills, so I returned to my job as a hired farmhand. Being an only parent, a mother who just gave birth, and working for only pennies a day to support me and my baby boy; I died not long after from exhaustion."

"What happened to Anthony?" Nic asked.

"A friend of mine took Anthony in, but he got the measles and died not too long after that," Shima said softly. "But I bet that Anthony would be just like you if he was older."

Nic smiled and nodded.

The two were silent for a second.

"Do you miss him?" Nic asked, "Your son?"

Shima smiled sadly, "Every day."

Nic looked at the counter avoiding eye contact.

"Nic, the point I want you to get is that I know this is not the life you wanted. But this is the life you got. You can do great things with this new life, or you can do nothing at all. I have found myself much happier in this life than in my old. I have lived for a long time and have seen such amazing things. I watched the nation battle itself in a civil war, I flipped on my first light switch, I saw the whole world at war twice, I rode in one of the first cars invented by Ford, I saw the nation become one, I am still witnessing the rise of technology and it's amazing." Shima said. "I want you to experience what I have and find what you like in the world. This is your choice." Shima counseled Nic.

Nic nodded, contemplating everything she said. "I just... from the moment I was born there was always expectations of me. They wanted me to be the best of the best. Zac was the oldest and my parents put all their pressure on him to succeed and they were overjoyed when he got accepted to Tempton University to study business finance. When my brother died, my parents stopped caring. They stopped pushing me, even though I pushed myself harder than ever before to succeed and make them proud. When I told them I wanted to go to Amington University to study music, my father didn't even argue against it. He thinks art schools are a waste of money, but he didn't even try to talk me out of it. They both didn't care. I guess, my point is that I need goals to achieve. I can't just live my life going from day to day in the hopes that something will happen. I need a goal to motivate myself to wake up in the morning and work hard."

Shima thought. "A goal huh?" She folded her arms and rubbed her chin. "If you still want to play music that is an option."

Nic nodded, listening.

"Was there anything in particular that you wanted to do with your music?" Shima asked, trying to help Nic.

"I just wanted to play. I didn't care what I was doing as long as it was with music."

"Then let's make music your goal," Shima said, "Maybe we can even record a few of your songs. A familiar's being and voice may not be able to be captured on a camera or a recording device, but the music can be. And who knows. Music varies differently in the magic world."

Nic was confused. "What do you mean?"

"There are special circumstances where you could even give live performances in the magical world."

Nic's eyes widened. "R-Really?!"

"Of course! They are always looking for entertainment."

Nic nodded and smiled. "That would be nice."

Shima smiled and rubbed Nic's shoulder. "Now that your goal is settled, onto other topics." Shima switched out of a motherly tone to a teacher with authority. "After school today, you will report directly to me," Shima instructed. "You are going to learn how to fight for the protection of yourself and your master." Shima glanced Nic over, "Where are your familiar weapons?"

"My what?" Nic asked confused.

Shima sighed. "Your daggers."

"Oh, those, they're in my room."

"Always wear them. They are enchanted to cut anything. As a familiar it is your duty to always be prepared, so you need to always be armed. Once you are done preparing Ash's breakfast, go to your room and strap those knives to your waist and keep them there." Shima instructed and stood up from her bar stool.

Nic looked at the counter once again.

"Nicky?"

Nic glanced up and paused as Shima kissed his forehead.

"You're doing great, keep up the good work." She whispered into his ear and walked out of the room.

Nic watched her leave. Shocked, he rubbed his forehead wondering if what just happened was even real.

Chapter 11

Nic balanced a tray of coffee with a beautiful short stack of blueberry pancakes as he walked to Ash's room. He knocked on Ash's bedroom door and waited a moment before entering. "Ash, it's time to wake up. You have school today." He reminded the wizard setting the tray on Ash's desk and walking over to the window. Nic opened the curtains to let the early morning sunshine in.

Ash moaned and rolled over in bed, trying to hide under the blankets, refusing to wake up.

Nic walked over to Ash's television which sat on the dresser and turned it on. Nic found the remote on top of the television and switched it from some a movie channel to a news station, hoping the noise would rouse his master out of bed. Nic looked at Ash to see him hidden under covers, trying to block out the barrage of light and sound. "I have breakfast prepared for you and it's getting cold," Nic informed his master as he picked up a little bit in Ash's bedroom, putting dirty laundry into the hamper.

Ash rolled over in bed and moaned. "Wasn't it just Sunday?" He muttered.

"Yep and now it's Monday; time to start the week over again," Nic said, finding a seat in Ash's rolly chair.

Ash pulled the covers tighter over his head.

Nic sighed and stood back up. "I can't make you do most things, but I do insist on one thing," He grabbed ahold of the covers and yanked firmly to rip the sheets off Ash which left him exposed to the bright and loud world, "Going to school," Nic finished.

Ash sat up. "Geez, what a wake-up call," He muttered, rubbing his eyes. "I look forward to waking up like this every day." Ash sarcastically sighed.

"As do I," Nic muttered unenthusiastically. Nic turned his back to his master to get Ash's breakfast tray.

Ash got out of bed and began to get dressed, pulling on a pair of gray cargo pants with a black t-shirt sporting a band's insignia on the front.

Once Ash was dressed, the wizard sat down on the edge of his bed and Nic set the tray delicately in his lap.

Ash slowly ate breakfast, which was really good.

Ash was quickly realizing how great of a cook Nic was. Shima was good at cooking, but Nic definitely blew her out of the water. "These pancakes are delicious."

"Thanks," Nic said, as he dug through Ash's backpack and sat in his rolly chair reading over Ash's Spanish homework, itching to fix the errors he was finding. A name caught Nic's ear and he looked up at the television as the local news reporter covered the car crash that took his life.

"Yes Janie," The reporter said. "Two vehicles were involved. The two victims were Amington high school students, Nicholas Russell and Trisha Roxwell. They were both admitted to the Amington Emergency Care Hospital with injuries. Trisha Roxwell was released with minor injuries including a gash on her forehead. But the driver, Nicholas Russell, was in critical condition after the accident and died while being transported to the hospital. Jessica Norton, the driver of the other vehicle is being charged with accidental manslaughter. It is said that Jessica sped through the intersection's red light as she was texting her boyfriend when she hit the other car. Jessica was not hurt but she is facing a penalty of a minimum of eight years in prison." Throughout the news report, the news station showed pictures of Nic's totaled car. Nic did not recognize his own car at first. The little silver car had every window busted, the driver door was ripped off along with the steering wheel, and the driver side was completely crushed inward. Nic felt sick once again when they showed a view of the driver's seat. It was like he was living it again and he remembered everything from the fear to the physical pain.

Ash wiped his mouth with a napkin. "Please turn the television off."

Nic obliged and hit the power button on the remote.

The two were silent for a long time, looking at the black screen of the television.

Nic returned to reading through the homework as if he never saw the news report.

Ash looked down at his breakfast, letting the silence of the room sink in. "I'm sorry about yesterday." Ash apologized after a long bout of prolonged silence.

"No," Nic said, closing the textbook. "I needed it. I shouldn't have responded like that. It was childish of me and you were only doing it for my best interest. I'm sorry."

"Nic, I understand and want to help you, if you will let me." Ash offered, noticing Nic was refusing to make eye contact with him once again.

Nic looked at the Spanish book in his hands. "I thought about it, about how I can never return to being human, and that bothered me all night long. Then, Shima talked to me this morning and it made me realize something. Even though I'm not human, I can still have goals and make achievements and do my best." Nic turned away from looking at the book and faced Ash. "Ash, I want to become your familiar. I want you to teach me. I will never be perfect, but it will give me something to strive for; a goal to try and accomplish. As I do that, I also want to work with music."

Ash smiled, "I think that is an awesome idea." Ash ate a bite of pancake and wiped his mouth with a napkin again, wanting a little dramatic flair. "I want to be the greatest witch doctor this world has ever seen, to do that I will need the ultimate familiar at my side. Do you think you can become such a familiar?"

Nic laughed and slowly bowed, making Ash's eye widen in surprise. "Yes, Master."

#####

Nic walked with Ash to school. The walk was not too long but Nic did not understand why Ash preferred to walk rather than drive to school. After all, Ash did have a fully functioning, decent-looking car.

As they neared Amington high, Ash looked at Nic. "I have some rules that you need to follow while I'm at school or any place in public."

"Like what?" Nic asked, looking at the sidewalk as he kicked a pebble out of the way.

"That!" Ash said pointing to the pebble. "Rule number one, don't touch anything."

Nic was confused. "Why?"

Ash thought of an example, "If you pick up a book or open a door, normal people will see a book floating in midair and a door opening on its own which isn't exactly a good thing." Ash enlightened. "If anyone were around when you kicked that pebble just then, they would've seen a pebble fly across the asphalt on its own."

"Okay, no touching, got it." Nic nodded.

"Second, please refrain from talking to me in public. I may accidently answer and the last thing I want to be labeled as is crazy, definitely during my senior year." Ash said, clenching his fists. "I made it this far keeping my life under wraps, the last thing I need is for you to be Mr. Talkative."

"So, no touching and no talking." Nic listed.

"And no going into the girls' locker room," Ash added.

Nic shook his head. "I can assure you that I will restrain myself." Nic guaranteed as they walked to school.

Ash walked through the main doors of Amington high, walking in with a crowd; Ash glanced at Nic to make sure he was okay.

Nic looked around flustered, he did not know what to do or where to move as people walked through him. Nic followed after Ash as the wizard broke off from the crowd and veered toward his locker. Nic walked through people, making it out the sea of people. "I hate this," Nic stated.

Ash fiddled with the lock and opened the locker, ignoring Nic. Ash dumped all of his textbooks inside and grabbed his books for his morning classes before locking his locker back up. He turned around and watched Nic trying to dodge out of the way of different students as they walked by. Ash said nothing to Nic and began to walk down the hall to Spanish class.

Nic followed close behind Ash but paused when he spotted something.

Ash walked a little further down the hall before realizing his familiar was no longer beside him. Ash spun around and retraced his steps, stopping when he noticed Nic standing before a locker. Ash approached and noticed that the locker did not have a door.

The door was taken off by the hinges and inside the locker were flowers, pictures, and sheet music.

"That's my locker," Nic said softly.

Guilt flooded Ash as he watched the familiar approach the locker, inside the locker was a picture of Nic smiling and holding a violin. Nic was dressed in a black suit with his hair neatly combed over for the senior band photo.

A girl strolled by with a single lily and passed through Nic to place it in the teen's locker.

Ash walked up to the locker and looked at it, inside the locker contained club photos and other pictures people had taken where Nic was the main subject. Many of the photos contained Nic and Trisha which Ash assumed Trisha had previously put within the locker. The sheet music within the locker was all from Nic's school folders, some of the music was even pieces which Nic had composed himself. There were other things like poems and song lyrics within the locker, but the flowers covered most of the things inside.

Nic gently touched the petal of the lily the girl just left for him.

"We need to go to class," Ash said softly, trying to tear Nic away from the sight of his locker.

With some persuasion from Ash, the familiar somehow managed to pull himself away and walked with Ash to Spanish.

Spanish and pre-calculus were the only two classes Nic and Ash had together, due to Nic being in the gifted courses. So it was a natural act for Nic to come to Spanish first thing in the morning. He walked in and looked at his desk. On Nic's desk was a framed picture of himself with a small bouquet of flowers laid beside it.

Ash glanced at Nic. "Are you going to be okay?" He whispered.

"Yeah, just give me a second." Nic said and walked over to his desk. Nic looked at the picture, almost forgetting that he was not supposed to touch anything when he almost picked up the picture frame to take a better look at the photo. The picture frame held Nic's senior class photo; he was wearing a suit and smiling like all seniors did.

Ash sat at his desk and watched Nic as a few more students walked in. Ash slowly realized how many people were wearing black. Even the Spanish teacher, Mr. Hernandez, wore a black polo shirt with off-color matching black jeans.

Nic walked over and sat on Ash's desk, waiting for class to start. "I don't like this," Nic mumbled.

"Today is going to be rough." Ash agreed, being quiet. Ash was trying to master the art of ventriloquism to talk to Nic without others seeing him. "How are you holding up?" Ash whispered.

Nic did not answer as he stood up off Ash's desk and walked over to the doorway.

Trisha Roxwell walked into class adorned in black. She had a giant bandage on her forehead and was walking with a slight limp. The promise ring Nic had given her was dangling on a chain around her neck. She had on thick eyeliner and her hair was down to hide her face as much as it could.

Nic walked over to her and gently touched her cheek, but she could not feel it. "Trish..."

Trisha's expression was very solemn, but she showed no signs of crying.

"Trisha." Nic whispered and reached out to take her hand, but his hand passed right through hers. "No, please just let me touch her," Nic begged and tried to touch her again, his hand phasing through Trisha's shoulder. Nic either phased through her shoulder or touched her without Trisha knowing. It frustrated Nic, making him want to scream.

A friend of Trisha's walked over and asked her how she was doing. Trisha only nodded, biting her lip. Trisha was refusing to cry. The friend hugged her and escorted Trisha to her assigned seat. A few more friends awaited the girl at Trisha's assigned seat to comfort her as well.

Nic watched and returned to Ash's side. "I can't do this," Nic confessed.

"Want to go back home?" Ash offered, he had pulled out his Spellcaster cards and was playing a makeshift game with them.

"But that's skipping." Nic sighed.

"I think this counts as a justified skipping." Ash said and played with his cards. "All you have to do is say the magic word."

Nic thought for a second. "Please?"

Ash quickly packed up his bag and slipped out before Mr. Hernandez began his lecture on conjugation.

Chapter 12

No questions were asked when Ash and Nic returned home early. Instead, when the two stepped through the doors they were each whisked away by their mentors. Ash continued his studies in potions with Uncle Jacob as Shima taught Nic how to fight.

It did not take Ash long to finish his potions lesson for the day, so he wandered about the house a bit. Thinking about his familiar, Ash walked up the stairs to the third-floor training room wanting to see how Nic was fairing against Shima. Ash arrived and opened the door to the training room.

The training room had a small area to lift weights, mirrors across the wall surrounded the room, a small bench against the wall served as a viewing area, but the rest of the room was empty with mats laid upon the floor.

Shima was in the middle of the matted area teaching Nic how to fight hand-to-hand as she promised earlier that morning.

To be honest, Nic was not very good at fighting and Shima was effortlessly cleaning the floor with him.

Ash walked over and sat in the viewing area as he observed the familiars' practice fights.

Presently, the two were running a full-paced sparring match. Nic could hardly get anything in with Shima coming at him so fast with a fury of punches and kicks.

Nic was wearing some gray gym shorts with a red t-shirt as Shima wore a navy blue spaghetti strap with tan shorts. Shima had her long black hair ponied up in a giant ponytail originating from the top of her head. She focused on teaching Nic with it whipping around wildly behind her.

Nic blocked a punch to his chest and followed quickly with a side step as she kicked at him. Shima recovered her footing and round house kicked Nic perfectly in the side of his face. Nic was stunned, the kick came at him too quickly and he had no idea how to block it. Nic fell hard to the ground and held his nose as a dark teal liquid poured out of it.

Ash noticed how it was the same teal liquid that was in the cauldron when Nic was made.

Shima tossed Nic a hand towel. "Clean up that bloody nose of yours. Blood will make the mats slick."

Nic held the towel to his nose. He had been sparring with Shima for hours now and this was not the first time he had been injured like this.

Ash walked over with his hands in his pockets and knelt beside Nic. "Shima is beating the living daylights out of you," He mentioned, regarding a pile of hand towels in the corner of the room containing copious amounts of teal blood stains on them.

"I keep messing up." Nic admitted and pulled the towel away from his nose to look at it. Deciding that the blood flow had finished, he bundled up the newly spoiled hand towel and threw it to add onto the pile of soiled towels.

"How are you feeling?" Ash asked.

"Like I'm getting my ass kicked." Nic sighed, tired.

"I meant, are you hungry?" Ash reworded his question.

Nic looked away, he was starving actually. Getting his butt handed to him by Shima was only making his hunger worse.

"A familiar's body is faster and stronger compared to any human, making them desirable in combat. But it requires nutrients to keep these advanced talents active. So before and after a battle, it's tradition for a witch or wizard to feed their familiar. Your movements are probably getting slower and that's because you're running on empty."

"Are you saying that I have to drink?" Nic asked, still catching his breath from the fight.

"I'm not saying anything. I'll wait until you are unconscious tonight after Shima kicks your ass a few more rounds or you can feed right now and jump back in rearing to go with a fair chance of improving." Ash offered.

Nic looked at the ground.

"Either way, I'm going to make sure my familiar is properly fed," Ash informed Nic, letting him know that there was no way out of this predicament.

Nic sighed and glanced over his shoulder at Shima who was working on a punching bag. "I'll manage on my own."

Ash raised an eyebrow. "You sure?"

Nic checked his nose again for blood, "Positive." He stood up and walked back into the center of the matted floor space.

Shima looked over from her punching bag. "Ready to go again, Nicky?" She asked, stretching and trying to warm back up.

"I am and it's Nic." He replied cooly and relaxed into a fighting stance Shima taught him.

Ash walked over to the doorway and paused, watching the fight between the two resume.

Nic was still fast, but Ash knew he could be faster with some blood.

It did not take long for Nic to miss a block and get kicked in the stomach.

Ash winced and left the two familiars alone as he walked out.

#####

After a few sparring sessions with Shima, Nic called it quits. His movements were getting slower as he tired out.

Nic returned to his bedroom to shower and dress in his uniform attire complete with his vest and tie. Afterward, he walked to the kitchen and was ordered by Shima to begin dinner preparations.

Nic looked around the kitchen and put together a homemade meal of vegetable lasagna. Nic whipped up a pan of lasagna and set it in the oven to cook. In his spare time, Nic started his other chores.

He walked to Ash's room and cleaned up as Ash sat on his bed playing video games. Nic felt like a slave as he walked Ash's dirty clothes to the laundry room and threw them in the washer along with the bloody hand towels he used during training. He put the detergent in the machine and turned it on.

Nic, then, walked to the living room. He had orders to dust, but Shima had it all taken care of.

He sighed, bored.

Nic had forgotten to remind Ash to pick up some new violin strings from the music store so he could restring his new violin. Thanks to their forgetfulness, Nic was left with nothing to do. He strolled over to the base of the stairs where a grand piano stood. He had been eyeing it ever since he first saw it during his solo exploration of the house before Nic realized that his life had been forever changed.

Nic pulled out the bench and sat down. He glanced up at the clock in the living room, checking the time. The lasagna would not be done for another half hour or so. Nic pushed back the cover of the keys and examined them. He played a few scales to test how well the piano was tuned. Surprisingly, it was well kept. He stretched his fingers and began to play.

Nic did not play any memorized sheet music or tried to recreate a melody he had heard before, he just played what he felt. His fingers danced across the monochrome keys playing a beautiful strong melody, but the flow was slow and held a sad underlying tone to its tune.

Jacob walked out of his study and stopped when he heard the beautiful melody. He followed the melody down the hall and stood at the top of the stairs to watch the young familiar play.

The melody rolled off in waves, sometimes the music was strong and almost euphoric, but for the most part, the song crashed down like a wave breaking against the shore into a soft melancholy tune. The music's melody came to an abrupt stop on a soft, sad note and Jacob watched as Nic only sat at the piano, fingers resting on the still keys as if contemplating to continue.

"You're not done," Jacob said.

The familiar looked up startled. He stood and bowed his head courteously. "I'm sorry. Did I disturb you?"

"No." Jacob chuckled walking down the stairs, hanging onto the banister. "I was merely in my study when I heard the prettiest melody. I couldn't help but come and investigate the sound. I was pleasantly surprised to find you playing this old thing."

Nic smiled softly. "She is a fine piano, but she's slightly out of tune."

"I will call someone tomorrow," Jacob assured Nic, standing before the piano. "But please, could you finish your song?" Jacob requested.

"That was it," Nic said with a small shrug.

"But it ended so suddenly," Jacob stated.

"Yeah, well, that was all that was coming to me." Nic sighed and sat back down on the bench and played a few more keys.

Jacob watched the teen familiar. "Nicholas, are you homesick?"

"Can't be homesick when you're already home," Nic said softly.

"You can when your heart hasn't arrived yet."

Nic was silent and played a key and let the note carry for a few seconds.

"It's a normal reaction for familiars to experience." Jacob sympathetically put a hand on Nic's shoulder. "You're doing a good job and I want to tell you that I'm proud of you. You have amazed me with your ability to adapt."

Nic looked up at Jacob and quickly returned to looking at the piano's keys.

"What can Ash and I do to help make you feel more at home here?" Jacob asked.

"I don't know," Nic confessed.

"You do. You're lonely," Jacob stated the problem without hesitation.

Nic said nothing; he touched a black key and let the note sing.

"Shima was just like you." Jacob laughed softly.

Nic looked up, interested, and scooted over as Jacob sat on the bench beside him.

"I was Ash's age when I created her; imagine my surprise when I not only got a familiar that was several years older than me, but she was a woman. At first, I didn't know what to talk to her about. She was this beautiful young lady who previously had a husband and son while I was this young farmer's kid with no ambition and a weird talent with magic. I lived with my mentor after I moved away from home and she lived with me. We became friends through studies."

"What do you mean?" Nic asked, intrigued by the story.

"Well, I taught Shima how to read and write. That was all I needed to do to find a common ground. We became the best of friends. We would read fairy tales to each other and invent impossible stories to entertain ourselves. When she cleaned I would even rant about my mentor's teachings and she would listen with full intent. Sometimes, we would escape from the house and go to the grassy field that was not too far away and watch the sky."

"You watched the sky?" Nic asked, in disbelief.

Jacob smirked. "We watched the sky, but I never remember looking at the sky if you know what I mean."

It did not click with Nic at first what Jacob was saying. "What did you look at?"

Jacob chuckled and winked, "You know the birds and bees, the flowers and trees."

"What?" Nic asked, confused by Jacob's cryptic explanation.

But before Jacob could say anything else, Nic's eyes widened with realization. "Oh! That!" He covered his face which was quickly turning red from embarrassment from not getting it sooner.

Jacob laughed heartily. "If talking doesn't work you can always try that way."

Nic's face was as red as his eyes. "I'm going to stick to talking."

Jacob laughed heartily and patted Nic's back.

Nic was wondering if it was possible to die from embarrassment as he covered his face to try and mask his blush.

Jacob chuckled, letting his fit of laughter die down. "Alright, I'm going to have Ash give me a tarot card reading."

"What for?" Nic asked, his blush successfully clearing away by the distraction of a new topic.

"I want to see how accurate the boy's skills are."

"They're pretty accurate," Nic said from experience.

"I take your word for it, but I'm going to investigate myself." Jacob walked up the stairs. He paused and looked back down at Nic. "I anxiously await to hear the end of that melody Mr. Nicholas."

Nic bowed his head. "Yes, sir."

Jacob smiled and walked up the stairs, leaving Nic alone with the piano.

Nic sat back down on the piano bench and played a few more keys.

Chapter 13

Four basketball players from Amington high were dressed in their finest black suits and ties. Their faces were solemn as they ever so gently pulled a wooden coffin out of the back of the black funeral hearse.

Almost everyone in Amington was at the gravesite, watching at the teens carried the coffin to the viewing destination. Once there, they gently lowered the casket down onto a platform and backed away to let the mourners view the coffin.

The front row seats of the viewing held Nic's entire family. Mrs. Russell sat with Mr. Russell, crying against his chest. Mr. Russell held his crying wife as he stared at the casket with a stone expression. Beside Nic's parents was Cassie, who refused to look at anything but the black sequins on her dress which she was currently picking at. The rest of the seats held Nic's aunts, uncles, grandparents, cousins, and closest family friends.

Nic and Ash stood among the mourners toward the back of the funeral tent. Ash was dressed in his finest, black suit and tie. Ash went all out, even taking the time to hair spray his ponytail and use bobby pins to pull his bangs out of his eyes so they would not cause a distraction. Nic and Ash watched as the pastor said some final words and invited everyone to come forward and say their final goodbyes. Nic's gaze shifted from looking straight forward at his family and his own casket to his right where the girl of his dreams stood.

Like on Monday, Trisha wore all black from head to toe. Even at Nic's funeral, she showed no signs of tears in her eyes. Trisha just looked at the casket, never shifting her gaze. Nic gently reached over and wrapped an arm around her, but as usual, she could not feel his touch or even knew he was there. Nic softly placed a tender kiss on her forehead and smiled sadly, watching her through the funeral.

Trisha suddenly walked out of Nic's embrace to proceed to the front of the viewing and placed a red rose on the coffin. Others followed her, placing flowers on top of the casket as well.

Once she placed her flower down and hugged each member of the Russell family, Trisha strode over to a nearby oak tree, outside of the viewing area.

Nic followed her and waited beside her as they watched his funeral begin to clear out.

Ash waited his turn to place a white rose on Nic's casket and pay his respects to Nic's family. Ash noticed the two under the tree and walked over to join them.

Trisha was silent, still watching the funeral as Ash stood beside her. The two were quiet for a long while before Ash spoke to try and break the tension. "Nic was a good guy."

Trisha nodded slowly.

"We use to be best friends in Kindergarten," Ash said, trying to make conversation.

Trisha said nothing, she only nodded.

Ash knew he needed something to break the ice. He thought for a bit, thinking of anecdotes about Nic and him. "We use to throw Legos at each other during nap time."

Trisha laughed softly, but the smile was sad and it did not last long as it quickly faded.

"The teachers couldn't turn their backs on us. We were horrible to each other." Ash laughed. "We use to make each other cry, but we were the best of friends."

"Why did you stop?"

"Huh?" Ash asked, not hearing her the first time.

Trisha cleared her throat in an attempt to become louder. "Why did you stop being best friends? If you were so close, why did you guys suddenly stop?"

Ash turned to look at Trisha who was now looking at him. Ash sighed and looked at the ground, staying silent for a long time. "We fell in love with the same girl."

Nic looked at Ash, shocked. Nic had been standing on the other side of Trisha the whole time, with an arm wrapped around her shoulders.

"We both liked you, but Nic was just faster. He was always better at socializing than me." Ash admitted, getting a little closer to Trisha.

"What are you doing?" Nic asked disturbed by the events unfolding before him.

Ash blew Nic off as he began talking about some of the adventures the two had, which only angered Nic. The more Ash talked with Trisha, the closer he got.

Nic backed off, astonished by what was occurring.

Ash eventually took over Nic's original position, wrapping his arm around Trisha's shoulder.

Nic was sickened, he felt nauseous. Was Trisha already moving on? Was Ash hitting on her? Was this really happening? And at Nic's own funeral?

Trisha did not appear to mind Ash's arm around her shoulder, she actually seemed to like it and drew a small bit of comfort from the gesture.

Nic shook a little, all he could think of was how this all could not be happening. "Get away from her!" Nic yelled at Ash. "You're moving in on her at my funeral?!"

Ash quickly shot Nic a look that asked him to please shut up.

Frustrated, Nic stormed away from the two. He could not believe what was happening. He walked back to his gravesite viewing, walking past or through everyone.

The viewing had, for the majority, cleared out but his family and a few friends still remained.

Right beside his future grave, was his brother's. Nic crouched down in front of the grave which read, Zachary Anne Russell. A fresh bouquet of white roses laid on his grave, most likely from his parents. Nic carefully picked a nearby daisy and added it to the pile. He looked at the tombstone for the longest time, silent, as he gently traced the letters of his brother's name that were etched into polished granite. "I wish I could've seen you again," Nic whispered.

"You do have that option." A female voice replied to Nic.

Startled, Nic spun around to see a beautiful woman with vibrant red hair.

The woman was gorgeous. Her red hair was curled with a healthy shiny luster that occupied each and every curl as they dangled just past her shoulders. She wore a completely black outfit consisting of a dress skirt, heels, and a sweater blouse. The woman's eyes were a lavender purple but were hidden behind a pair of reading glasses. Around her neck was a silver necklace with a skull charm dangling off it. She held a small black purse which she dug through and pulled out a tiny black book. She carefully opened it and flipped through a few pages. She smiled after stopping on the desired page, "Here you are." She carefully coughed to clear her throat. "Nicholas Tanner Russell. Died: November 12th at 7:48 pm. Cause of Death: blood loss due to a car accident. Family life has been unstable since the death of beloved brother, Zachary. Love life was established, but future goals were not yet achieved. Special notes: Familiar to Ashton Starnes." The woman looked up from her book with lovely light violet eyes. "You are Nicholas, I presume?"

"Yes," Nic answered, standing. "May I ask who you are?"

"How polite," The woman mused, "My name is Cherri." She smiled softly.

"H-How can you see me?" Nic asked; amazed to finally talk to someone else who could see him beside the Starnes family.

"I am here to ferry your soul into the next world Nicholas, for I am a grim reaper."

Nic backed up a step. "A grim reaper?" Those very words sent a shiver down Nic's spine by just hearing them.

"Yes. Please don't be afraid." Her words were so calm; they hypnotized him, making him want to trust her. "Your time has come. You are no longer needed in this world."

"What about Ash?" Nic asked.

"This is not about Ashton, this is about you, Nicholas. What do you want?" Cherri kindheartedly asked the young familiar.

Nic looked at the grave, thinking. What did he want? He looked up at the reaper who stood just outside of arm's reach of him. She was smiling kindly at him as he pondered. "I want to see my brother," Nic confessed.

Cherri offered her hand with a gentle smile. "Come with me and I will take you to him."

Nic looked at Cherri's hand and reached out to take it.

"Nic, get away from her!" Ash ordered.

The white of Nic's eyes were consumed by black as the red irises glowed. Nic retracted his hand and backed up promptly.

Cherri clicked her tongue annoyed and turned to look at the young wizard.

"I never thought I would see the day when reapers would stoop so low as to try and harvest the souls of changeling familiars. How desperate can you get?" Ash sneered at the reaper and stood in front of Nic protectively.

Cherri pursed her lips and pushed her glasses up. "I guess I'm going to have to do this the hard way."

Ash smirked. "You don't scare anyone. Even with your death scythe, you wouldn't dare to fight in such a populated area, nor could you take on a wizard and a fully energized familiar."

The more Ash regurgitated logic, the harder Cherri's icy violet glare became.

"Fine," She snapped. "But I will return for his soul eventually."

"Yeah, yeah," Ash muttered, turning his back on her. "Come on Nic, we're going to walk Trisha home."

The reaper looked at Nic. "I will be back for your soul," She warned Nic with a sly smile.

Nic nodded solemnly. "I understand."

"Farewell Nicholas. We will meet again." She smiled and waved as black mist engulfed her.

Nic watched amazed as Cherri disappeared before his eyes. He then focused and returned to Ash's side. "Hey, can I ask you a favor?" Nic asked, walking beside Ash

Ash was silent, ignoring Nic once again as they walked back to the tree, passing through the viewing.

"Can you go easy on Trisha? It was almost like you were flirting with her." Nic said, accepting that Ash could not afford to look at him all the time or it would compromise Ash's established sanity amongst his classmates.

Again, there was no answer from Ash, not even a glance over as an acknowledgment.

Nic was getting frustrated. "I just want someone to listen to me and acknowledge my existence!" He yelled at Ash and was completely blown off once again as Ash offered to walk Trisha home.

Trisha accepted Ash's offer with a slight nod.

The gray sky rumbled threatening the world below with impending rain.

Ash briskly walked Trisha home with Nic sulking behind them. The two talked all the way to Trisha's house, a few times Ash was able to wrestle out a ghost of a smile from Trisha's protected emotions. Trisha was heavily guarding her emotions making sure nothing slipped out accidentally.

Ash walked Trisha up to the front door and the two said their goodbyes.

Trisha thanked Ash for walking her home and waved to him briefly as she disappeared inside.

Ash waved back and glanced over at Nic, "Ready to return home?"

Nic did not reply, he only crossed his arms and began the trek home with Ash following right beside him.

Chapter 14

Ash and Nic did not speak a word to each other as they walked home.

Ash could sense that Nic was upset, but there was nothing he could do to relieve that. What all Ash did was comfort Trisha. Sure he knew that he ignored Nic, but it was necessary for people to not think that he was insane.

Nic opened the door for his master and closed the door behind them.

"Nic, I just want to say," Ash started, ready to apologize even though he knew that he was not in the wrong.

"Whatever you have to say, I don't want to hear it. Just leave me alone." Nic huffed, walking past Ash, never making eye contact with the wizard. Nic stormed into the kitchen and turned the stove on. The familiar filled a pot with water and set it on the warming burner.

Ash followed Nic to the kitchen and watched the familiar begin dinner preparations. "Nic, please listen to me. It's not what you think."

Nic pulled out some vegetables, washed them. He then chose a knife from the knife block and began to slice the vegetables up as he completely disregarded Ash.

"I don't know Trisha like you do. You and Trisha were really close, so she's in a lot of pain right now. I was just trying to comfort her and show her that I'm someone she can confide in and talk to." Ash shielded himself with the truth.

Nic grit his teeth as he continued to chop vegetables. "You were very touchy-feely to only be comforting her," Nic muttered, never bothering to look up from chopping up the vegetables.

"She needs comfort. She just lost her best friend!" Ash argued.

Nic bit his tongue and stabbed the knife into the cutting board in his anger. "What a load-! You were moving in on her!" Nic yelled accusing Ash. Nic muttered a few things to himself and left the room, trying to get away from the wizard.

Ash followed, refusing to be shaken off so easily.

Nic walked to the laundry room and pulled out Ash's bed sheets from the dryer and folded them neatly to set in a hamper.

"I was not moving in on her." Ash denied, blocking the only entrance and exit to the laundry room.

Nic continued folding laundry, trying to overlook Ash as much as he could. "Ash, I don't wish to discuss this anymore."

"We barely discussed anything!" Ash huffed frustrated.

Nic finished the laundry and picked up the hamper to walk by Ash. "I just want to do my chores and get away from you."

"What's your problem?" Ash questioned, refusing to let Nic through.

Nic glared at Ash, clenching his teeth. Nic looked away, refusing to say anything.

"You have been moody since the day you woke up a familiar! What do I have to do to prove that you're dead?!" Ash yelled at Nic. "No one can see you! You no longer belong to the human world! You need to get the illusion that you are still a living human out of your thick head! You're a familiar! My familiar! And you need to damn well start acting like it!"

Nic dropped the hamper, spilling the clean folded laundry all over the floor. "You made me this! I never wanted to be a familiar!" Nic yelled back in retaliation at Ash, before turning away.

Ash watched as Nic shook a little. Nic's eyes were covered by his black hair as he looked at the floor. Ash could still see Nic's chin and he watched as tear droplets collected on the familiar's chin to fall. Ash's eyes widened, realizing what horrible things he yelled at Nic.

Nic covered his face. "I'm stuck watching Trisha every day. She's so depressed because of me, and the worst part is that she will never see me or feel me or even know I'm here and exist! Do you know what that's like?! Do you really?! I love her and could do nothing as I watched you put your arms around her today." Nic was shaking and his voice was starting to crack.

Ash could tell that Nic was trying to hide the fact he was crying.

"I can never talk to her again, or hold her, or tell how much I love her. She's going to grow old and I'm going to be stuck looking like this, forever! I'll never be able to be with her!" Nic sniffed and wiped his eyes. "And you made me like this," Nic whispered the last part, which Ash was barely able to hear.

    Ash's world slowed to the point where everything was still. Was he really the root of all this? The reason Nic was a familiar was completely his fault. Ash performed the spell to bring a compatible soul to the brew. Was it fate? From the day Ash was born, was he destined to have Nic as his familiar? Was the only reason Nic was born, was to die and become a familiar? Was it fate that caused the car crash which took Nic's life? If Ash never wanted to make a familiar, would Nic still be alive? A lump formed in Ash's throat as his stomach churned. What if he truly was the root of everything? Because of Ash, Nic returned from the dead as a familiar. Ash took away Nic's chances of being with his big brother in the afterlife. Ash was the cause of all of Nic's pain and suffering. Even now, he hurt Nic once again by just being able to talk to Trisha. Ash hung his head and stepped aside from the doorway to let Nic by.

    Nic wiped his eyes and carefully walked past the wizard. Once he was past Ash, Nic ran down the hall to the front door. He slammed the front door behind him as he ran outside.

    Ash stood in a depressed trance fearing that he was the cause of all of Nic's misfortune.

    A loud 'Thwack' rang through the house as Ash stumbled forward suddenly, head throbbing. "Ow!" He whined, holding the back of his head and looking behind him.

    Shima held a feather duster, which she used to hit Ash upside the head.

"What was that for?!" Ash demanded.

"Being a jerk," Shima replied, dusting the picture frames in the hall.

"I wasn't being a jerk." Ash denied, crossing his arms.

"You made Nicky cry." Shima glared at Ash. She folded her arms in front of her chest which pushed up her breasts.

Ash looked way, examining a painting in the hall so he would not have to make eye contact with Shima. Ash tenderly rubbed the back of his head where he was hit. "So?"

"Nicky is trying as hard as he can, I would be mad too if I saw you touching my lover at my funeral," Shima said rather pissed off. Shima dusted a tiny table which held a landline phone and a lamp.

"I was no-," Ash started to defend himself, but Shima cut him off.

"I, frankly, don't care what you thought you were doing. You are in the wrong here. Nicky shouldn't have reacted the way he did, but you are the master. And as the master, you need to set the example and be the better man."

"But..." Ash tried to argue.

"Is that sass I'm hearing?" Shima hissed, her eyes flashing red and black.

Ash shut up immediately. "No ma'am."

"Good. Now go and get your familiar, the color box says that it's about to storm outside. The last thing I need is for you two to come into my clean living room, soaking wet and covered in mud. I refuse to clean that mess up." Shima said and returned to her dusting.

Ash walked down the hall and his hand rested on the door knob, thinking. He looked at the woman familiar, "Do you believe in fate?"

Shima smiled softly. "I do."

Ash nodded.

"You better hurry and bring Nic back," Shima smiled sweetly. "Because your fate is waiting to kick both of your asses when you return." Shima crossed her arms, expressing how angry she was.

Ash laughed nervously, "Thanks, Shima." He closed the door behind him.

Shima sighed and returned to her cleaning.

Ash opened the door again and popped his head back inside. "Oh, by the way, I love you, Shima. But just for your information, that 'color box' is called a television."

"Shut up and look for Nic!" Shima yelled at the young wizard about to throw something at him.

Ash laughed and walked out onto the front porch, assuming that Nic could not have gone far definitely with the brewing storm. "Nic?" He called, looking around and not seeing his familiar anywhere. "Nic!" Ash called louder, but still he saw nothing. "Nic!" He ran down the walkway and looked around, it started to sprinkle and he was getting concerned. Nic was nowhere to be found. "Nic!" He looked down the road and cupped his hands to his mouth. "Nic!" He yelled as the rain poured down in unrelenting sheets.

#####

Nic ran down the sidewalk, he had to get away from Ash, he did not care where he went as long as Ash was not there.

It had just started to rain, and he was soaking wet. Nic was freezing, the icy rainwater and the fall November air only made it worse. He slowed down as he approached Trisha's house. Nic stood in front of the house and looked up at a window on the second floor.

The light was off in Trisha's room upstairs and the curtains were pulled closed.

Nic walked up the steps of the house and stopped. He thought for a minute and shifted into his animal form.

A black dog now stood in Nic's place. The dog shook off his soaking wet fur and looked up at the door. Nic whined and scratched at the front door.

After a few minutes with no one answering the door; Nic threw his head back and began to howl, begging to be let in.

Chapter 15

Trisha laid in bed, the curtains closed, the lights off, and all the doors locked. A single lamp illuminated a small corner of the room beside her bed. She held her phone and looked at the background picture of her and Nic at a carnival.

Nic was holding Trisha as she held a stuffed bear that was almost as big as she was; Nic won it for her at the carnival. The two were both smiling and having fun. Trisha looked at the picture and skimmed through more on her phone. She had a picture of Nic sleeping in Spanish class, Nic playing piano during the school-sponsored talent show, Nic dressed as Frankenstein and Trisha dressed as Mrs. Frankenstein for Halloween, and numerous other photos on her cell phone. Trisha wanted to smile and reminiscence in the happy memories. Every single time she tried, she remembered that she would never have those memories again with Nic.

Trisha's phone vibrated as someone texted her. She quickly checked it, hoping it was Nic and all of this was just one stupid nightmare. But the message was from a friend of hers named Bethany. Trisha ignored the message, it was only going to be a sympathy text and she had enough of those already. No one ever talked to her, but now that Nic was gone, it was like everyone remembered she existed and wanted to talk to her. Trisha did not want sympathy; she just wanted everyone to leave her alone. Nic was gone and he was not coming back.

The worst part to this tragedy was that it was all her fault.

If Trisha's car did not break down, she would have just driven herself home. It was Trisha's fault for everything that occurred. She was the one who did not get her engine checked for such a long period of time, and she was the reason her car broke down. Trisha was the reason why her car had to be kept in the auto shop. Trisha was the reason Nic wanted to take her home, and she was the reason why Nic died. Nic would be alive right now if it was not for her. This was all her fault, Nic's blood was on her hands and no matter what she did, she knew she could never scrub it off.

Trisha looked over at the promise ring Nic had given her the day of the accident. It was sitting on her nightstand, she wore it every day since the accident. She sat up and gently picked up the little silver ring and held it to her chest.

She wanted to cry, it probably would make her feel better, but she could not. She felt horrible guilt as she blamed herself for Nic's death. She wanted to cry so badly, but mentally she knew that she did not deserve to cry.

Trisha pulled her hair to the side and carefully put the necklace on, struggling for a second with the tiny clasp. She wore her promise ring and walked over to her desk by the window. She picked up her sketchbook from her desk and returned to her bed.

After the accident, Mr. Russell hand-delivered Trisha's backpack and sketchbook which was saved from Nic's car before it was towed to the junk yard.

Trisha sat down with the sketchbook and opened it to skim through the pages. A few pages stuck together with dried blood from when Trisha's forehead cut dripped on it in the car. Thankfully, none of the drawings were ruined.

Trisha looked at each picture, the entire book was filled with sketches of Nic. Nic playing a collection of instruments, playing basketball during physical education, reading in class, driving, and a wide assortment of other pictures with Nic as the focal point. Trisha opened her nightstand drawer and pulled out a fine line pen, wanting to go over some of the drawings to darken them.

There was a soft knock on Trisha's door.

Trisha carefully bookmarked the page she was on with the pen and stood. She walked over and unlocked her bedroom door.

Trisha's mother stood at the door with a cup of raspberry tea. "I made you some tea. I was thinking, maybe we could talk?" Mrs. Roxwell offered, handing her daughter the teacup and saucer.

Mrs. Roxwell looked just like her daughter, except older. The woman had lighter brown curly hair which she always wore in a pony with a headband. Mrs. Roxwell wore glasses which shielded her brown eyes and she could always be seen wearing jeans and pastel blouses.

"I don't want to talk about it, mom," Trisha said, looking down at the steaming cup of tea her mother gave her.

"It will make you feel better." Mrs. Roxwell coaxed.

"No mom. It won't, it will only make it worse." Trisha whispered.

"Okay," Mrs. Roxwell said softly and kissed her daughter's cheek. "I love you."

"I love you too mom." Trisha smiled sadly. "Thank you."

"No problem dear. What do you want for dinner?" Mrs. Roxwell asked.

"I'm not hungry."

"I will ma-," Mrs. Roxwell paused as howls rang through the house. "What on earth?"

Trisha heard the howls too, she set the cup of tea on her dresser.

Mrs. Roxwell walked downstairs, followed by her daughter as they investigated where the howls were coming from.

The howls grew louder as they neared the front door.

Trisha looked at her mother, silently asking her what that noise was.

Mrs. Roxwell shrugged and looked through the peephole in the front door and smiled. "Well, it looks like we have a guest." Mrs. Roxwell opened the door, but a glass screen door was still there to provide a barrier between them and the wet black dog on their porch.

The dog whined and begged as he pinned his ears back, tail wagging.

"Have you ever seen this dog before?" Mrs. Roxwell asked Trisha.

Trisha tried to remember, but the dog did not look like any of the neighbor's dogs. "He has a collar on, maybe there's an address or a vet's number we can call."

Mrs. Roxwell opened the door a crack, and the two slipped out onto the porch.

The dog's tail wagged and his ears perked up as he looked up at Trisha.

Trisha bent down and gently pet the dog as Mrs. Roxwell read the tag on the collar. "There's an address and the other side has his name."

Trisha scratched behind the dog's ears, making his tail wag faster. "What's his name?"

"Nic." Mrs. Roxwell answered.

Trisha's hand froze for a second before she continued to pet Nic. "Hi, Nic. You're a good boy."

Nic's tail wagged and he licked her cheek.

"What do we do with him?" Trisha asked.

"He has to be lost, poor thing. We need to just keep him for the night, we're supposed to get some pretty heavy storms and I wouldn't feel right leaving such a good dog on the front porch. We can keep him in the garage until the storms clear out." Mrs. Roxwell proposed.

Nic's ears fell and his tail stilled, he did not come to Trisha's house to sleep in the garage.

"Trisha, I'm going to find the address in the phone book and call the number, can you give him a bath?" Mrs. Roxwell asked.

Trisha nodded. "Come on boy." She whistled and led Nic inside. She walked to the bathroom as Nic padded close behind her. Trisha closed the door behind them, locking Nic inside the bathroom. She sat on the ledge of the bathtub and began to fill the tub with warm water as she watched the black dog wander about.

Nic smelled around the bathroom, it smelled just like Trisha's house. She always had a unique sweet spicy smell like pears and cinnamon. In his animal form, the smell was intensified with his heightened senses.

Trisha gently pet Nic as he walked over to look into the tub which was filling quickly with bathwater. She carefully removed his collar and set it on the counter. She turned the bathwater off when the tub was full and opened the cabinet below the sink. "I think I still have some canine shampoo from my dog Scooter." She found the bottle and pulled it out. "I think you would've liked scooter, he was a chocolate lab," She said talking to the dog before her, scratching under Nic's chin.

Nic remembered Scooter; he was a good dog but died a year ago from old age.

"Alright, you need to get into the tub mister," Trisha said, rolling up the sleeves to her sweater.

Nic's tail wagged and he walked over to the edge. He smelled the water first and then gracefully jumped over the edge into the warm bath water, splashing the water about. The hot water felt amazing, definitely since Nic was still chilled to the bone from the cold rain water. Nic barked and his tongue rolled out the side of his mouth.

Trisha smiled softly. "You're a silly dog; I've never had a dog that actually liked to take a bath." She informed Nic and tied her hair up. "Now let me get you cleaned up." She poured a few cups of warm bathwater over Nic before uncapping the bottle of dog shampoo and pouring it along Nic's back. She then lathered the shampoo into Nic's black fur.

Getting his fur washed felt so good, almost like a massage. Nic wagged his tail, excited and accidently made the water slosh in the bathtub, splashing Trisha.

Trisha gasped, shocked that Nic splashed water on her.

Nic's tail stilled and his ears pinned back as he whined an apology.

Trisha let out a small laugh. "Jerk, you weren't supposed to give me a bath."

Nic smiled, tail wagging, as he licked Trisha's face.

Trisha giggled. "Okay goofball, let me finish bathing you." She resolved and continued to scrub Nic.

After she finished, Trisha drained the bath tub and let Nic jump out.

Trisha hastily threw a dry towel over Nic before he could shake off. She moved quickly and worked on drying Nic off with the towel. Trisha then pulled out a hair dryer from a drawer and uncoiled its cord before plugging it in and turning it on. Trisha sat on the toilet and used the hair dryer to continue drying Nic. She ran the dryer over Nic's fur coat, finger combing the silky black fur and untangling the small knots she would come across. "You're a good boy." She cooed and scratched under his chin.

Nic licked her face.

"I like you too." She smiled softly and finished drying Nic off. Once Trisha was finished, she let Nic out of the bathroom. Trisha walked to her room and closed the door behind her, but Nic had already slipped in. She turned around and watched as Nic jumped onto her bed and made himself comfortable, lying down. "Do not get too comfortable there, even Scooter wasn't allowed on my bed."

Nic barked defiantly and Trisha rolled her eyes.

A scent tickled Nic's nose, it was the scent of blood. He sniffed the air, trying to track the scent. His nose led him to a purple sketchpad on Trisha's bed which Nic identified as the source of the smell.

Trisha walked out of her closet, finding a t-shirt to wear and saw Nic smelling her sketchbook. She shoed Nic away and picked up the book. "That's not for you." She scolded and put it on her dresser where he could not reach it. With the book in a safe place, Trisha decided to get out of her wet clothes. Trisha stripped off her top.

Nic's eyes grew wide.

Under the black sweater top was a spaghetti strap, but Trisha was undressing in front of him. She went to take off the spaghetti strap and he turned his head, looking away.

If he was human, he would have been completely red.

Nic glanced over to see if she was done.

Trisha had on a new black shirt, but now she had no pants on. Nic's eyes grew wider after seeing her panties and he looked away once again.

Trisha put on some pajama bottoms as her mother called, "Trisha dear, dinner's ready!"

Trisha pet Nic, "Does food sound good to you?"

Nic wagged his tail and barked before jumping off Trisha's bed and following her down the stairs to the kitchen.

Trisha walked to the kitchen with the black dog at her feet.

Mrs. Roxwell handed her daughter a plate of cucumber sandwiches. "I called the address. He belongs to a man named Mr. Starnes. Mr. Starnes thanked us and asked if we could keep him for the night during the storm."

"Starnes? Like Ash Starnes?" Trisha asked, recognizing the name.

"I don't know. I talked to a man named Jacob and he seemed nice." Mrs. Roxwell cut off a piece of pork chop and dropped it on the floor for Nic, giving him a treat.

Nic looked at the piece of meat, tilting his head.

"You okay boy?" Mrs. Roxwell asked.

Nic knew he could not eat human food like that and not expect himself to vomit. Nic carefully took the pork chop piece and held it in his mouth without swallowing.

"Good boy." Mrs. Roxwell scratched behind Nic's ears as Nic walked around the kitchen.

Nic felt like he was going to vomit as he held the rancid-tasting pork chop piece on his tongue, looking for a place to dispose of it.

"I will make up a spot in the garage for Nic."

Nic stopped when he heard Mrs. Roxwell. He quickly hid the piece of meat under a counter and returned to Trisha's side, ears dropped unhappily.

"That won't be necessary," Trisha said softly.

Nic's ears perked up.

"I want him to sleep in my room tonight," Trisha admitted.

"Oh, okay." Mrs. Roxwell nodded. "I'll bring some towels and a toy up for him."

"Thanks, mom." Trisha smiled and looked at the dog. "Come Nic."

Nic followed Trisha upstairs to her room and jumped back onto Trisha's bed.

Trisha smiled softly. "Yeah, you better get comfortable." She set the plate of sandwich halves on the dresser beside her, now cold, cup of raspberry tea. Trisha laid on the bed beside Nic.

Nic smelled her face and she gently pet him. He licked her cheek making her smile and giggle softly. He curled up to her and nuzzled her face as Trisha looked over at her phone.

Trisha picked up her phone and checked to see if she had any new messages. There were three, but they were all from her friends. None from Nic and there were never going to be any. She sighed and cleared out the messages. She looked at Nic and pet his soft fur.

Nic whined and looked at her phone.

"I just want him to text me and tell me this is all a dream," Trisha said softly.

Nic whined and nuzzled her face.

Trisha petted him. "I want to wake up from this nightmare," She whispered.

Nic barked and whined.

Trisha hugged Nic, burying her face into his soft, warm fur. "It's my fault," She whispered, "I want him back so bad." She whispered against his neck.

Nic wanted to hug her and tell her that everything was okay and that she would be alright. His shoulder suddenly felt warm. He looked over to see Trisha shaking softly. Nic gently laid his head on her shoulder as she cried.

Chapter 16

Trisha's phone alarm rang, signaling that it was time for her to wake up and get ready for school.

Nic woke and looked at Trisha, waiting for her to turn the alarm off which was irritating his sensitive ears.

Trisha had fallen asleep against Nic and was slowly rousing awake as she picked up her cellphone. With a swipe of the screen, the phone was silenced. Trisha yawned and gently pet Nic.

Nic yawned and stretched. His stomach growled, telling the rest of his body that he was hungry.

Trisha held her phone and looked through her messages. Seeing nothing new from Nic, she laid down the phone and scratched Nic behind his ears.

A soft knock interrupted the monotonous rhythm of Trisha's fingers through Nic's fur.

Nic lifted his head off his paws and looked up at the door.

"It's not locked," Trisha informed the knocker.

Mrs. Roxwell entered with a cup of tea and a muffin on a little silver tray. "Hi," Mrs. Roxwell smiled. "I made you breakfast." She set it on the nightstand beside her daughter's bed, noticing the untouched tea and sandwiches on the dresser from the night before. "Are you going to school today?" She asked softly, trying to talk to her daughter.

"I really don't want to," Trisha admitted with a sigh.

"Then you don't have to go." Mrs. Roxwell allowed, giving her daughter permission to skip. She gently pushed a strand of hair behind Trisha's ear and kissed her daughter's forehead. "I love you."

"I love you too mom." Trisha smiled sadly. "Thank you for breakfast."

Trisha knew she would not eat breakfast, but it was the thought that counted.

"I'll be back to check on you later." Mrs. Roxwell informed her daughter and left her in peace, closing the door behind her.

Nic rolled on the bed and curled up to Trisha.

Trisha smiled and pet him. "Good morning, Goofball." She laid there still for a while, petting the black dog before slowly getting out of bed. Trisha walked over and retrieved her sketchbook from atop of the dresser. She returned to sit beside Nic and opened the book, finally showing Nic what was contained within the sketchbook's pages.

Nic was stunned to see that the book was comprised of nothing but sketches of himself. Each picture held so much detail, it was amazing. He watched as Trisha traced over each line with her pen, darkening the lines and making all the details of the drawing become more prominent. Nic never knew what Trisha was always drawing, but now it was right in front of him. He smiled and licked Trisha's cheek.

Trisha laughed softly and pet the black dog.

#####

Ash slumped down into his desk and yawned, it was only first period and he was exhausted. Ash had stayed up a good majority of the night running down the streets during the horrendous storm calling out for Nic.

After braving the storm, Ash returned home yesterday empty-handed and scared that something horrible happened to Nic. First thing Ash did after returning home was was rush to the potion room and gather the ingredients needed to perform a summoning spell. He was going to call Nic home while Shima yelled at him about tracking mud everywhere. During the ritual process of making the spell, Jacob walked in and informed Ash that Nic was safe at the Roxwell residence.

Ash sat in his seat thinking about how furious he was at Nic for running away. But at the same time, Ash was scared. The wizard had to make sure that his familiar was okay, it was his job as a master to ensure that Nic is always safe and healthy.

Ash watched the door, sitting in class. If his plan works, when Trisha goes to school Nic will follow. But the bell eventually rang for first period to begin which signaled for Mr. Hernandez to get up and begin drilling his Spanish class with vocabulary flashcards. Ash sighed as Trisha did not show up for class. The wizard diverted his attention to the lesson and listened.

#####

Mrs. Roxwell knocked on Trisha's door in the evening, holding a phone with her hand over the mouthpiece. "Trisha, there's a boy on the phone; he says that he's the owner of the dog."

Trisha looked up from her sketchbook, currently working on a draft sketch of the dog sleeping beside her. She set the pencil behind her ear and pet Nic. "Come in."

When the door opened, Nic woke up and raised his head.

Mrs. Roxwell walked over with the phone and gave it to Trisha.

Trisha took the phone, covering the mouthpiece. "I will bring it down when I'm done," She promised her mother.

Mrs. Roxwell understood and left Trisha alone, closing the door behind her.

Trisha put the phone to her ear. "Hello?"

"Hi Trisha, this is Ash Starnes." Ash greeted.

"Hi, Ash."

The knot in Nic's stomach grew and he whined.

"Shhhh." Trisha shushed the dog and gently pet him.

"Your mom said that you found my dog," Ash mentioned.

"Yep. A black husky-wolf mix?" Trisha asked, scratching behind Nic's ears making him wag his tail.

"That's him. He ran away from home last night and I was looking everywhere for him, my Uncle said that you found him."

"Yeah, we found him. He was in the storm for a little while, but we cleaned him up and kept him nice and warm. He's a good boy." Trisha said, still petting Nic.

Nic barked, letting the wizard hear him over the phone, and smirked smugly as Trisha continued to pet him.

"Can you put me to Nic's ear for a second?" Ash asked Trisha.

"Uh… Okay." She replied, thinking that it was a little odd, but she did it anyway. She put the phone to Nic's ear.

Nic was nervous about this as he listened, whining to show that he was there.

"Listen here wonder dog, you need to come home and drink blood before you get too weak to function." Ash lectured over the phone line.

Nic huffed through his nose; basically telling Ash, 'Hell no'.

Ash was about to scream Nic's ear off, but Trisha put the phone back to her ear. "Your dog is adorable."

"Oh, yeah. Well listen," Ash said, trying to think of the proper way to say this. "I would like to come over and pick him up tomorrow if I can?"

"Of course, you can come with me after school," Trisha suggested.

"Yeah. Sounds like a plan." Ash said. "Thank you for taking care of my dog."

"No problem." Trisha smiled.

"Bye Trisha, I'll see you tomorrow."

"Bye Ash."

"See you tomorrow Nic," Ash said over the phone, knowing that Nic could fully well hear him.

"Nic says bye." Trisha smiled, scratching behind Nic's ears.

Nic huffed again, 'no I didn't' was all he thought as he listened to Trisha and Ash's phone conversation.

"Bye Ash." Trisha repeated and hung up. Trisha placed the phone on the nightstand and returned to petting Nic. "Such a good boy," She whispered and took the pencil out of her hair to continue sketching the dog.

Nic curled up beside her and drifted back to sleep as she pet him.

Chapter 17

Nic woke up and stretched. He sat up and a wave of nausea hit him hard, making him lay back down. He felt horrible. Nic's stomach churned with nausea, his head pounded with a throbbing headache which was currently making him lightheaded, and his throat was so dry that it felt like in any second it would start cracking and crumble into dust.

Trisha's phone alarm started to sing, signaling that it was time for her to get up. Trisha groaned and picked up her phone. She swiped the screen, switching the alarm off and laid in bed for a few more minutes before forcing herself to sit up and stretch.

Trisha looked at the black dog beside her and pet him. "Hi, Nic." She smiled at the dog.

Nic's tail wagged, weakly.

Trisha stood up and walked to her closet, picking out some clothes for school before going to the bathroom to change and brush her teeth.

Nic stood on his paws. He was shaky and so hungry. He needed to eat, but he could not face Ash just yet.

Moments later, Trisha walked out dressed in a black sweater and a lacy black skirt with colorful galaxy leggings and black flats.

Nic watched the girl he liked from atop the bed as Trisha prepared her backpack for school. Nic whined and rolled onto his back.

Trisha glanced up and smiled softly. She reached over and rubbed Nic's belly. "You be a good boy while I'm gone."

Nic rolled over and barked a reassurance.

Trisha situated a bowl of dog food and water in the corner of her room for Nic before leaving. She closed the door behind her and walked down the stairs.

With Trisha out of the room, Nic focused and shifted into his human form.

He felt much better in his human form. The nausea was alleviated, but he was still so hungry. He brushed the feeling off and straightened his uniform, fixing his tie and vest before phasing through Trisha's bedroom door and following Trisha to school.

#####

Ash sat in Spanish class, once again paying attention to the door when Trisha walked in. Just as Ash predicted, following close behind her was his familiar.

Nic glanced at Ash and for a second the two made eye contact. The eye contact hold did not last long as Nic looked away, breaking it to follow Trisha to her desk in the corner.

Class began and Ash watched as Nic stood beside Trisha throughout the lecture.

Nic was paler than normal and had dark bags under his eyes, courtesy of not eating in two days. He was also shaking, it was slight, but Ash could see it. Nic's body was starving and the familiar was doing nothing to help it.

A familiar's body was like a human's. Blood is as important as water, without it familiars become terribly weak and very ill. In a worst case scenario, they could even die. But typically the instincts of a familiar would force the familiar to submit to their bloodlust and feed from their master before it ever got to that point.

Just by looking at Nic, Ash could see how bad Nic's predicament was but at least it was not dire.

"Mr. Starnes?" Mr. Hernandez called out.

Ash looked forward startled, switching his attention from his familiar to the teacher in front of the classroom. "Huh?" He asked, not knowing why his name was being called.

Everyone in class giggled, laughing at the teen wizard's reaction.

"No, the answer is not 'huh?'." Mr. Hernandez mocked. "Please stop staring off into space and focus on the lesson. We are on page 159 in the textbook, please open it up and follow along." Mr. Hernandez scolded the teen and returned to the topic of present perfect conjugation.

Ash opened his book, glancing at Nic before focusing his attention on the foreign language.

#####

Ash typically ate his lunch by himself on the patio outside under the metal awning. Ash never minded eating alone, he liked the peace. He always ate his bagged lunch in his corner typically reading a book he brought with him or sometimes people would want tarot card readings and he would happily oblige for a price.

But today was different, Ash was on a mission.

Ash never went into the cafeteria. The cafeteria smelled of fried mystery meat, overcooked vegetables, and teenage pheromones. As the students conversed with other students, the building became filled with the sounds of screaming laughter and the rolling thunderous boom of voices making the cafeteria unbearable to be in by Ash's standards. Ash looked around for Nic, whom he had not seen since Spanish class that morning.

Trisha was in the gifted track just like Nic, which meant that Ash shared no extra classes with her. Ash caught a glimpse of Nic last period during physical education, but he did not get a good opportunity to actually talk to him since he followed the girls to play matt ball in the gym while the boys were forced to play flag football outside.

Finally, Ash spotted the familiar at a table of popular girls. Trisha was sitting at the table conversing with a few of her friends while Nic stood behind her like a well-dressed bodyguard.

Nic's eyes widened, seeing Ash approach and he looked away as if he did not see the wizard.

Ash sighed and under his breath, he muttered an order, "Come to the bathroom."

All orders were absolute, even if they were barely spoken over a whisper.

Nic's eyes glowed red and black. He sighed and trudged to the bathroom where Ash stood waiting by the sinks. Ash waited with his arms crossed and sported a look of disapproval.

"What?" Nic sighed, sticking his hands into his trouser pockets. He knew he was in trouble, but he did not care. He just wanted to hear whatever Ash had to say and return to Trisha.

Ash did not answer for a while as he only surveyed his familiar. "You," Ash replied.

"Me?" Nic raised an eyebrow and crossed his arms, ready to argue with the wizard.

"Nic, why are you doing this to yourself?" Ash asked, exasperated.

"What are you talking about?" Nic asked, blowing it off and acting like he was perfectly fine. He turned the water on at a sink and washed his face.

Ash grabbed Nic's shoulder and spun him around to face him. "You're shaking like a little dog, you're as pale as a ghost, pardon the expression," Ash excused himself for the slip of the tongue, "And you have bags under your eyes."

Nic knocked Ash's hand aside. "So?"

"You're starving."

Nic's stomach growled at the very thought of food.

"I understand if you don't want to come home." Ash sighed. "I'm not going to make you, but if you aren't coming home tonight, please take some of my blood." Ash insisted and rolled up the sleeve of his jacket to offer his arm to Nic.

The white of Nic's eyes were consumed by black as the irises glowed red. His eyes locked sights on a thick, juicy blue vein running up Ash's arm. Nic licked his lips as his stomach growled, he was so hungry. Nic hissed and grabbed Ash's arm. He brought it to his mouth, licking the area.

Ash prepared for the sting of Nic's fangs, but it never came.

Nic's eyes reverted back to their blood red color making Nic release Ash's arm. "No!" He backed away from

Ash. "I don't want it." Nic gasped, trying desperately to suppress his familiar instincts.

"You're being stupid!" Ash yelled at Nic.

"Leave me alone!" Nic shouted back as a breeze came from nowhere, making the paper towels flutter in the dispenser and the bathroom stall doors sway. He stumbled back, his head feeling very light.

Ash caught Nic's arm, saving the familiar from falling down. "I don't want to order you to drink Nic, but so help me I will." Ash threatened.

Nic's red eyes glared into Ash's blue eyes, daring the wizard.

Before Ash could say anything a student walked into the restroom to use the urinal.

Nic glared at Ash and shrugged off his hand. The young familiar stormed out, knowing Ash could do nothing with the other teen in the bathroom.

Ash cursed his luck and followed. He ran out of the bathroom, but Nic was nowhere to be found.

#####

Jessica's two friends, Amy and Claire, sat at Ash's desk before pre-calculus listening as Ash gave each of them a tarot card reading about their future. Ash was still watching the door, and noticed the minute Trisha and Nic walked in.

Trisha walked over to Ash's desk, with Nic behind her, and waited as Ash finished Amy's fortune.

The two girls paid Ash and returned to their seats, talking about the results of their fortunes.

Ash looked up at Trisha and smiled. "Hey, Trisha. How are you?"

Trisha timidly sat down in the seat across from Ash. "You wouldn't believe how many times people have asked me that today," Trisha mentioned, looking down and never meeting the wizard's eyes.

Ash did not think of that, he assumed more than he could count.

"I've had people I don't even know or talk to come up and ask me that." Trisha sighed.

"I'm sorry Trisha. Can I do anything for you?" Ash asked.

Trisha smiled sadly. "That's always the second question asked."

Ash felt like an idiot, he had the urge to face palm but he withheld it. "Then why don't we talk about something else?" Ash suggested.

"Well, I wanted to make sure that we were still on for you picking up your dog after school today?" Trisha asked quietly.

Ash quickly glanced at Nic, who seemed intent on ignoring the wizard and was currently looking out the window. Ash glanced back at Trisha. "I'm sorry. But something came up after school today and it's really urgent, I can't cancel or reschedule or I would." Ash apologized.

Trisha's eyes widened in astonishment. "Oh, well..."

"I'm so sorry to impose and I know this is an inconvenience to you, but can you keep him another night?" Ash asked.

Nic looked at Ash, surprised by what he was actually doing.

"Don't worry about it Ash. I love your dog," Trisha smiled softly. "Nic is a big sweetheart. My family can put him up for another night." Trisha responded, relieved. Honestly, Trisha was not emotionally ready to give the dog up just yet. Nic was very therapeutic to her in this time of loss.

"Thanks. How's your head?" Ash asked.

Most of Trisha's cuts and bruises she received from the crash had healed, even the gash on her forehead was not as bad now that it was scabbed over.

"It still hurts." She disclosed, touching the bandage on her forehead tenderly.

"It will take time to heal." Ash nodded.

"I know," Trisha said, thinking about everything, "But... I just want the pain to die."

Ash stood from his desk and gently hugged her. "Physical pain may take a few days or weeks to recover, but emotional pain may take a lifetime to recover. Just know that it's okay to cry every once in a while. Time is the ultimate healer of all wounds, but tears are a great temporary pain reliever." He comforted, whispering into her ear so no one else could hear. "I know you miss him. You loved him dearly, more than anyone. And I know that he loved you the exact same way."

Trisha bit her lip, holding everything in and tried to swallow the growing knot in her throat. She pushed Ash away gently and covered her mouth, no one had ever talked to her like that. "E-Excuse me." She choked and ran out of the room.

Nic watched her run out. The familiar glanced at Ash before following Trisha.

#####

Trisha ran into the girl's bathroom and Nic followed, hesitantly. No one was in the bathroom at the moment and Trisha fell to the floor on her knees. "Nic..." She whimpered softly, trying her best to still keep the tears in, but they were coming out by force. Trisha gasped, choking on her sobs.

Nic crouched down beside her. "I'm here." He whispered and rubbed her back, but Trisha felt nothing from the contact.

Trisha pulled out her cellphone and called her mother.

The phone rang for a bit until her mother finally answered.

"M-Mom, can you p-pick m-m-me up?" Trisha managed to say between sobs. "I-I-I want to go h-h-home."

Mrs. Roxwell panicked hearing her daughter crying over the phone and promised to be over faster than Trisha could blink.

Trisha hung up and pulled herself off the bathroom floor. She staggered over to the mirror and examined herself. Her eyes were red and puffy from crying, and she felt so stupid. All Ash said was a few sentences, but it was enough to send her into a fit of tears. Trisha felt like such a weak idiot. She washed her face in one of the sinks and tried to dry off with a paper towel. It was a pathetic attempt to cover up that she was previously crying.

Nic left her alone for a second to return to the pre-calculus room.

Mrs. Sandra was going over homework which Ash had not done and had no intention of doing. As Ash listened completely bored, he watched as Nic phased through the door of the classroom and looked at Trisha's book bag on the floor.

Nic wanted to pick it up and carry it out; but an invisible being carrying a backpack out is kind of scary, almost as scary as if Nic tried to drag it out. Nic thought and thought, looking at the bag.

Ash stood and raised his hand.

"You okay, Ash?" Mrs. Sandra asked, looking at the typically quiet teen sitting in the back corner of the classroom.

"Actually, I was wondering if I could take Trisha's bag to her. She ran out of class not feeling well earlier."

Nic looked at Ash, stunned.

"Goodness." Mrs. Sandra gasped. "Yes, take her bag to her and tell her to check out poor thing. I will email her the homework assignment."

"Will do." Ash grabbed the two textbooks on Trisha's desk and picked up her backpack before following Nic out the room.

Ash walked with Nic silent for a while as they walked down the empty halls.

With classes in session, everything was pretty quiet and no students lingered in the halls.

"Thank you," Nic said, glancing over at Ash.

"No problem." Ash shrugged it off.

"No, seriously, thank you. I would've never been able to get that bag out if you didn't help." Nic thanked Ash.

"It's seriously not a problem," Ash said and walked alongside Nic. "Now, where's Trisha?"

"She was in the girl's bathroom when I left."

Ash stopped walking. "Dude, you went into the girl's bathroom?"

"Yeah?" Nic shrugged like it was no big deal.

"Dude! What part of no girl's locker rooms do you not understand?!" Ash said a little too loud and quickly lowered his voice.

"I didn't go into a girl's locker room; I went into a girl's bathroom. There's a difference." Nic argued his claim calmly without changing his stoic expression.

Ash shook his head. "Barely." The wizard muttered and followed Nic to the girl's bathroom.

Nic passed through the door to check on Trisha. He returned a few seconds later, "She already went to the drop-off/pick-up center."

Ash nodded and walked with Nic down the halls and out the double doors.

Trisha was sitting on a bench under the metal awning, looking at her phone as the two boys walked out. She glanced up at Ash and rubbed her eyes, making sure they were dry and hoping they did not look too red and puffy.

Ash handed Trisha her two textbooks and her backpack.

Trisha's eyes widened with surprise. "Thank you, Ash, that's really nice."

"No problem, didn't want you to leave your stuff. Mrs. Sandra also said to check your email tonight, she's going to send you the assignment."

Trisha smiled softly. "Thank you," She repeated.

"Hey, it's no problem; call it even for taking care of my dog tonight." Ash shrugged.

Trisha nodded. "Still, thank you." She set the two textbooks down on the bench and nervously gave Ash a friendly hug.

Nic unhappily watched, as Ash received the hug and contact he craved for.

Ash wrapped his arms around Trisha to return the hug as a blue SUV rolled into the drop-off/pick-up center.

Trisha broke the hug and picked her books back up. "That's my mother."

"Well, I guess I'll see you tomorrow," Ash said.

"Yeah," Trisha agreed and her eyes suddenly widened. "Oh! Ummm... I almost forgot." Trisha looked up at Ash. "I'm actually having a party at my house tomorrow, it's my birthday, and I was wondering if you possibly wanted to come pick up your dog and stay for the party?"

Ash thought about Trisha's invitation and rubbed his chin. "I'll be there. It will give me another excuse to pick up my dog."

Trisha giggled quietly. "Thank you again, Ash."

"No problem." Ash waved as Trisha walked over to the SUV.

Trisha gave Ash a small wave and opened the door of the SUV to climb in.

Nic got in the back seat, phasing through the door to sit behind Trisha and her mom.

The scene oddly reminded Ash of the ghostly hitchhikers in the Disney *Haunted Mansion* ride.

Ash waved, as the car pulled away from Amington high. "See you tomorrow," He said softly and returned to class.

Chapter 18

Mrs. Roxwell pulled the blue SUV into the garage and the automatic garage door closed behind the vehicle as Trisha and Mrs. Roxwell got out of the car. Mrs. Roxwell fiddled with her keys and tried to unlock the back door.

Nic slipped by the two and phased through the door, beating Trisha inside. He ran up the stairs and passed through Trisha's bedroom door as Mrs. Roxwell finally managed to unlock the back door.

Nic quickly shifted into his dog form and waited for Trisha on the bed, tail wagging. Nic was getting weaker; He felt drained like he ran a marathon.

Trisha walked to her room and opened the door.

Nic greeted Trisha on the bed, tail wagging.

Trisha dropped her school bag onto the floor and flopped onto the bed beside Nic with a moan.

Nic curled up to her, tucking his tail around his body.

Trisha smiled as she gently pet the dog beside her.

Nic loved how Trisha ran her slender fingers through his thick black fur. He yawned, exhausted from all the running around at school. The familiar rested his head on his paws and drifted in and out of sleep before finally passing out on Trisha's bed.

#####

Nic was typically a light sleeper, but that was not the case that Thursday night. Nic slept through everything when he finally woke it was Friday morning.

Trisha was sleeping beside him and her phone alarm was singing. Trisha moved and scratched behind Nic's ears as her phone alarm kept ringing. "You up, sleepyhead?"

Nic looked around. He felt horrible just being awake, and he knew that he was getting worse. Nic was so weak, it drained him to so much as move. He laid still and whined softly.

Trisha looked down at the dog. "You okay Nic?"

Nic whined again as an attempt to tell her he was fine, but it came out as a pained whimper.

"Mom!" Trisha called, detecting that something was very wrong with Nic.

It took a few minutes for her mother to answer, but she finally did. "What is it?"

"I think Nic is sick," Trisha said, gently petting Nic's thick black fur.

"Sick?" Mrs. Roxwell walked up the stairs to her daughter's room and entered. She carefully looked Nic over as he laid still, refusing to budge.

Trisha got dressed for school as Mrs. Roxwell examined the sickly dog.

"I don't think it's anything serious. I just think his tummy is a bit upset. Did he eat too much yesterday?" Mrs. Roxwell asked her daughter.

"He didn't eat at all, his dog bowl looks untouched," Trisha said, pointing to a corner where she put a dish of food and water out for Nic yesterday when she left the dog alone in her room.

"Did he eat something he wasn't supposed to?" Mrs. Roxwell asked.

Trisha shook her head, "Nothing that I've seen."

"Hmmm..." Mrs. Roxwell thought. "Well, we're just going to let him rest. I am sure that it's just gas or something, it will pass over. If he gets any worse, we'll take him to Dr. Morrison."

"Thank you, mom," Trisha said, finishing getting dressed by putting a black t-shirt on with her jeans.

Mrs. Roxwell hugged her daughter, "Happy birthday."

Trisha smiled and hugged her mother back. "Thanks."

"Your father told me to tell you happy birthday as well."

"Will he be back home for my party tonight?"

"No, he has another conference tonight." Mrs. Roxwell explained.

Trisha sighed, understanding that her dad had to work but still wishing he could have been there for everything, for Nic's passing.

Trisha's mother smiled. "He has a flight back to Amington first thing in the morning. He told me to tell you that he's sorry and he will do whatever you want tomorrow as an apology."

Trisha smiled softly. "Sounds fun."

"Okay, Birthday girl. Don't have too much fun today at school, you will have to save some for the party tonight."

"Yes, mom." Trisha laughed quietly, grabbing her school bag and walking out with her mother.

Once Mrs. Roxwell closed Trisha's door, Nic tried to sit up. He stopped midway, there was too much pain shooting through his body. Nic laid back down and panted. He closed his eyes and slowly shifted back into his human form; it took less energy to be in that form.

As Nic laid there and looked up at the ceiling, watching the ceiling fan hypnotically spin; he found himself closing his eyes and drifting back to sleep.

#####

Nic woke to the sound of the front door opening. He looked at the green neon-colored clock on Trisha's wall; it read four o'clock.

Nic quickly shifted back into his animal form. He was still very weak, but the nap helped curb the pain a little.

Trisha walked in and pet Nic. "How are you doing boy?"

Nic licked her hand and Trisha giggled. "Feeling a bit better I see." She set her book bag down and walked over to her closet. "I need to help mom get ready for the party tonight," She explained, mostly to herself as she picked out a sundress to wear.

Nic looked away and gave her some privacy as she changed.

Trisha put on a green dress with brown swirls. She ponied her hair up and swept the bangs over to the side. Trisha changed out her earrings from silver buds to dangly green leaves that matched her dress perfectly.

Nic looked at her nightstand, noticing for the first time that the promise ring he gave her was there. He trotted over and picked up the necklace by its chain. Nic then returned to his place at the end of the bed and whined, holding the necklace by its chain in his mouth.

Trish turned to look at Nic when the dog whined. She gasped and carefully took the necklace away from Nic. "Oh, be careful with that!" She scolded the dog.

Nic pinned his ears back and whined an apology.

She gently held the promise ring. "I forgot to wear it today."

Nic nodded and tilted his head to the side as he watched Trisha's eyes tear up.

Trisha sniffed and tried to wipe her eyes. She carefully attempted to put the necklace on, but she was having difficulty with the tiny clasp.

Nic wished so much that he could help her with the necklace, but that would require opposable thumbs which dogs majorly lacked.

Trisha looked in the mirror and smiled. She turned around to Nic. "Ta-da!" She twirled, showing off her outfit to the black dog. "What do you think?" She asked.

Nic could not respond in any understandable replies, so he barked with his tail wagging excitedly.

Trisha opened her bedroom door and Nic followed her down the stairs to the kitchen.

Mrs. Roxwell was busy trying to finish decorating the house, "Trisha dear, can you hand me those scissors?" She held up a banner and pointed to a pair of purple scissors on the kitchen counter.

Trisha picked up the scissors and handed them to her mother as Nic looked around the Roxwell house.

The Roxwells were animal lovers and the entire living room was African safari themed with animal prints, earthy tones, and a lot of wooden furniture. But presently the living room had green streamers and party balloons everywhere; there was even a banner that read 'Happy Birthday Trisha!' among other decorations.

Mrs. Roxwell had been decorating all day and was almost finished, which was good since the party started in less than an hour. "Trisha, can you help me get the food out of the fridge?"

Nic followed and sat to the side as Trisha and her mother pulled out different bowls of dips, snacks, finger foods, and numerous other treats that Mrs. Roxwell had already prepared in advance and had waiting in the fridge wrapped in saran.

A buzzer rang, stinging Nic's sensitive ears.

Mrs. Roxwell turned the buzzer on the oven off and removed some pigs in a blanket on a cookie sheet.

Nic smelled the air. The aroma made his mouth water and his stomach twist up, he was starving. Nic walked over to sit by the dining room table where Trisha was removing saran wrap from dishes and arranging them systematically around the table. Wherever Trisha went, Nic followed.

Mrs. Roxwell looked at Trisha's little black shadow and laughed. "He's a keeper."

Trisha nodded sadly, "Unfortunately he belongs to a classmate of mine."

Mrs. Roxwell sighed. "You knew we couldn't keep him."

"I know," Trisha exhaled. "And it's horrible to say, but I was hoping that his owners abandoned him or something," Trisha confessed looking down at Nic.

She really wanted to keep him. Nic had helped her a lot through this week of hell after losing her Nic in the horrible car accident.

"I've been telling your father that we need a companion around the house. It's been quiet around here since Scooter died." Mrs. Roxwell said and gasped. "Why don't we go to the adoption center tomorrow and we see if we can find you a dog or cat?" Mrs. Roxwell beamed at her own suggested idea, already excited about the proposed plans.

Trisha nodded slowly, that was not exactly what she wanted but maybe a pet of her own would keep her mind distracted from other things, like Nic.

Mrs. Roxwell scooped the pigs in a blanket off the cooking pan and onto a plate with a spatula, accidentally dropping one which landed right in front of Nic.

Trisha looked over noticing her mother drop the finger food. "I can't tell if that was intentional or if you're just clumsy." She teased her mother.

"I may have a soft spot for the dog too." Mrs. Roxwell admitted.

Nic smelled the dropped pig in a blanket, looking it over carefully.

Trisha smiled. "We need to be careful mother. I don't want to spoil Ash's dog."

"It's only one." Mrs. Roxwell smiled and winked at her daughter mischievously.

Trisha sighed and laughed, "Mother!"

Nic picked up the pig in a blanket in his mouth and carried it to the laundry room, trying not to look suspicious.

When in the privacy of the laundry room, he set down the finger food and eyed it suspiciously. He felt sick just looking at it. The nauseous feeling he was getting reminded him of the time when he had the flu in middle school, just looking at food then made him sick to his stomach.

Nic sniffed the pig in a blanket. He wanted to eat it so badly.

As a human, Nic loved Mrs. Roxwell's cooking; but everything was different now, human food did not exactly agree with him.

Nic looked at the finger food. The longer he looked at it, the hungrier he became. He finally decided to bite the bullet. Nic did not care if it made him worse, he knew in his mind that he had to take the gamble. He scooped up the pig in the blanket and tried to eat it.

As he chewed, everything tasted wrong like his taste buds had been rewired. The cooked flesh of the wiener tasted like burned rubber and the crispy pastry dough tasted like dry, flaky clay. Nic spit up the finger food, it was awful.

The familiar sighed and returned back to the kitchen where Trisha was helping her mother fill an ice chest with sodas. Nic walked over and sat, waiting for Trisha to acknowledge him.

Suddenly the doorbell rang, announcing that the first party guest had arrived.

Chapter 19

    Ash wore a black dress shirt accompanied with a red tie. He highly doubted he needed to wear such formal clothes to a birthday party, but Shima insisted and would not let the wizard leave the house until he met her dress requirements.

    Once Ash was out of the house and walking down the sidewalk to Trisha's, he untucked his black dress shirt and loosened the necktie. Ash was not going to Trisha's to party, he was fetching Nic and that was all.

    It worried Ash that Nic did not even attend school with Trisha today and it only made him antsy to get over to Trisha's house and investigate why.

    Trisha's house was not too far, so the wizard decided to walk and forwent driving his car. As he approached the Roxwell residence, he noticed the numerous cars lining the sides of the streets and was thankful for not driving; parking would have been a problem.

    Ash was surprised with the crowd. He was kind of embarrassed to admit it, but he had never really been to a party before. The last time Ash went to anything even remotely resembling a party was in middle school when some Spellcaster fans invited him over to play. Unfortunately, Ash kicked their butts so badly they never invited him again, and that was without even using magic.

    Ash loosened his already loosened tie and rang the doorbell. He could hear catchy pop music blaring inside and waited patiently at the door. He was just beginning to wonder if it was acceptable to just walk in when Trisha answered the door.

Ash blushed and smiled, "Hi."

Trisha looked beautiful in a slim-fitting green sundress. The brown swirl patterns on the dress reminded Ash of the curls in her hair which were contained in a cute ponytail with her bangs pinned to the side. "Welcome, please come in." Trisha smiled shyly, inviting Ash inside.

Ash took her up on the invitation and entered, looking around.

Almost everyone in their senior class was there. They all loitered about, some danced with the music, others were at the dining table eating some snacks, some were in little clusters talking amongst themselves, and others were jumping from group to group socializing. Ash stuck to Trisha, looking around but not really wanting to socialize with anyone in particular.

"Can I offer you anything to drink?" Trisha asked. "Soda? Punch? Water? There's also food on the table if you're hungry."

"No thank you, I ate before I came," Ash said, not spying Nic anywhere. "If it's no trouble, I would like to see my dog."

"Oh, he's in my room. But," Trisha looked around like she was uncomfortable just being in her own house. "Can I talk to you first?"

"Sure, I guess." Ash shrugged, it was hard to hear her over the booming music and the thundering conversations taking place in the background.

Trisha motioned for Ash to follow her. She led him onto the porch and opened a screen door that leads outside to her backyard.

Ash's eyes widened with amazement. Trisha's backyard looked like something out of a movie. There was a huge wooden gazebo in the middle of the yard with a pretty stone and flower garden surrounding it. String lights were strung across the yard overhead, making them look like stars in the night sky. Ash whistled, "Wow."

"My mom is a professional outdoor landscaper," Trisha explained wringing her fingers nervously.

"No kidding." Ash looked down at pond filled with koi fish as they crossed the bridge to get to the gazebo. The entire place was gorgeous, just like it was pulled out of some type of dream.

They ambled over to the gazebo, walking along a wooden pathway. They climbed the steps of the gazebo and Ash continued looking around amazed as Trisha leaned against the banister.

From outside they could barely hear the music, much less the conversations of the other party goers. "It's so beautiful out here." Ash complimented.

"Thanks, I thought this would be a little easier to speak, it's kind of crowded inside."

Ash chuckled. "Yeah, a little too crowded for my tastes."

"And mine," Trisha admitted, looking down at her hands as they played with a corner of her dress.

Ash cleared his throat and looked around. "So, what did you want to talk to me about?" Ash asked, looking at Trisha.

"It's Nic," Trisha admitted.

"Is something wrong?" Ash asked, getting concerned.

"I just wanted to tell you first before showing you. He's not feeling well; he looked a little sick today." Trisha disclosed.

Ash sighed, relieved. "Yeah, figures." He muttered under his breath but said it a little too loud.

"He hasn't eaten much," Trisha added, "We made sure to provide him with plenty of food, but he just refuses to eat."

"Sorry. I should've said something. He's a picky eater." Ash apologized.

Trisha nodded and added softly. "I also wanted to thank you for letting me keep him for the few days. He has helped me a lot this week."

Ash reached into a pocket of his cargo pants. Even with the formal attire on, he refused to wear anything but his black cargo pants.

From his pocket, he pulled out a white box tied closed with a purple string and presented it to Trisha. "I got this for you as a birthday gift and a thank you for taking care of my dog."

Trisha took the little box, it was not wrapped but the little purple string tied to it really pulled it together to make it pretty. She carefully untied the string's bow and removed the lid. Trisha gasped softly and pulled out a heart-shaped locket on a silver chain.

"I know this will sound dumb, so don't quote me and mock me later." Ash coughed, clearing his throat already red with embarrassment. "I saw this in the store and thought if you put a picture of Nic inside then you could keep him close to your heart. I know that sounds romantically sickening, but I thought you would like it." Ash wanted to face palm realizing how stupid he sounded.

Trisha looked at the locket and bit her lip. She put the locket back in the white box Ash gave her, never saying anything or even looking at him.

Ash looked at the ground, rubbing the back of his neck nervously. "You don't like it, do you?"

He was suddenly hit hard in the chest as Trisha hugged him. She buried her face into his dress shirt as she hugged Ash tightly.

"Thank you, so much," She whispered, tears collecting in her eyes which Ash could hear in her whisper.

Ash smiled softly and gently hugged her back. "Trisha, it's okay to cry," He said softly, gently rubbing her back in calming circles.

Trisha bit her lip as she held back tears.

Ash smiled sadly, "Nic still loves you and he always will. You need to know that he loves you with all his heart." Ash did not know what else to say to Trisha as he held her against his chest.

Trisha bit her lip harder, making it bleed as a single tear could not be held back and ran down her cheek.

"Nic was a great guy and you need to remember that. Nic always loved it when you smiled, so he wouldn't want to see you cry, definitely not on your birthday. Am I right?" Ash asked.

Trisha refused to look up. If she did, it was guaranteed that she would start to cry. She hated people seeing her cry, it made her feel weak. "Yes," She whispered, knowing that she was stronger than this.

"Nic is watching over you and he's closer than you think."

Trisha looked up at Ash, finally revealing her hazel tear filled eyes. "Thank you."

Ash hugged her, resting his head on the top of her's. "No problem."

#####

Nic felt horrible, he was pretty sure that he was dying... again.

The music downstairs was giving him the worst headache, drilling into his sensitive hearing to try to split his head open. His hunger was growing by the second as his stomach clenched and his throat began to feel more and more like a parched desert.

Nic paced the room in his human form, getting antsy. The familiar saw movement out of the corner of his eye and looked out the window to investigate. Trisha's window had the best view of the backyard and Nic watched as Ash strolled alongside Trisha to the gazebo.

Nic observed the two as they talked for a bit, able to hear fragments of what they were saying with his advanced hearing. He watched as Ash gave Trisha something which quickly turned into hugging.

Each passing moment only made Nic angrier at Ash.

Nic focused and tried to tune out all the music to listen to the two in the gazebo. He listened intently, anger rising then cooling down as he realized Ash was not moving in on Trisha. Guilt flooded him as he heard Ash even talk Nic up.

Nic sighed, he felt so stupid.

"Pretty heart moving, huh?" A female voice commented.

Nic jumped, startled by the voice. He looked to his right where a woman stood beside him with vibrant red hair and black clothing.

The woman glanced at Nic. "Remember me?" She asked with a small smile.

Nic remembered, "You're the woman from my funeral, the grim reaper."

The reaper looked slightly different. Her hair was no longer curled but straightened and fell to the middle of her back. She wore a black blouse and black dress slacks instead of a skirt. She carried the same black handbag draped over her shoulder and extracted the tiny black book from within it. She held the book with one hand as the other hand fiddled with her silver necklace that held the skull charm on it.

"I do have a name you know." The woman informed Nic as she flipped to a specific page in the book.

Nic thought for a few seconds. "Cherri," Nic said, finally remembering.

Cherri looked up at Nic surprised. "Wow, I think you are the first familiar that actually remembered a reaper's name. I'm impressed."

"Your hair is red like a cherry," Nic explained his rationality of names.

Cherri laughed, "How simplistic."

"Why are you here?"

"To collect your soul," Cherri answered, very high-spirited.

"What?" Nic gasped, stumbling back. "No." He refused.

"Oh sweetie, you don't get that option." Cherri blocked the only exit out of Trisha's bedroom, besides the window. "As a reaper, it's a disgrace to let a soul go free without being collected. I gave you four days to sort out all of your worldly problems, now it is time for you to come with me. I have been more than generous."

"I don't want to go."

"As I said earlier, you don't have a say in this." Cherri informed Nic and sighed. She walked over to Trisha's full-length mirror and examined herself in it, fixing her red hair. "Being a reaper is a simple job and I've always had a perfect track record. I finish my book and then I start a new one; collect a soul, ferry the soul, stamp the soul collection page, and then the page disappears to be filed by office reapers. You were the only soul to ever get away from me." Cherri informed Nic.

Even though she wore a smile, Nic could see and feel the hate emanating from her light violet eyes which were partially hidden behind her glasses.

"Your page sullies my book, mocking me with the knowledge that I still haven't collected your soul, but all that changes tonight. You're too weak and your master isn't here to save you." She finally stopped fiddling with her necklace. Swiftly, Cherri grabbed the necklace by the skull charm and yanked it off, exuviating a bright blue light which illuminated the darkened bedroom.

    Nic covered his eyes for a brief second and watched as the broken necklace in her hand extended and grew into a scythe. The light faded and she stood before Nic wielding a glinting, silver scythe which was almost twice as big as she was. On the tip of the staff was a skull that was the size of an average adult skull, giving Nic a size comparison on the scythe's blade which was more than twice as big as the skull. "I'm clearing my book tonight." She informed Nic and swung her death scythe at the familiar.

Chapter 20

Nic fell to the floor as the scythe swung over him, narrowly escaping the sharp blade. He watched it, knowing that it had to get stuck in the wall giving its enormous size, the breadth of the swing, and the power behind the blade. There was no way the reaper could possibly stop it, it was basic physics.

But Nic's theory was proven wrong, nothing stopped the scythe as it phased through the wall.

Nic hit the ground and scrambled back to his feet. "H-How can you do that?" Nic asked shocked, pointing from the scythe to the wall in a panic.

Cherri smiled. "My scythe will only touch souls and nothing else unless I will it."

Nic panted already exhausted.

"Nicholas, I only want to save your soul. Come with me."

"No." Nic panted, catching his breath.

"We are the same, Nicholas. We are beings that don't belong in the human world. You don't belong in this world." Cherri offered her hand to Nic. "Come with me. Let me take you to your brother."

"My brother died a long time ago." Nic muttered, reaching behind his back to where his familiar weapons were strapped to his waist. "And I'm not ready to follow yet!" Nic yelled, unsheathing a dagger and throwing it at her; imitating how Shima threw the kitchen knives.

The dagger hit and buried into Cherri's shoulder. She screamed, more startled than hurt.

Cherri looked at her shoulder where the dagger laid embedded. She sighed and looked at the familiar bored. "Nice try Nicholas, but how about we aim next time?" She frowned and yanked the dagger out of her shoulder, and dropped it onto the floor. "Strong little weapon, enchanted to be lethal to any spiritual creature if hit in a vital spot."

Nic held his other dagger by the hilt, ready to unsheathe it if she so much as tried to approach him. Nic shook, his vision was getting a little blurry.

"Give up Nicholas, you can't beat me. I know you're weak from hunger." Cherri said, twirling her scythe around.

Nic panted and smirked. "You're right. But I could still beat you, with or without blood!" Nic yelled, pulling the dagger from its sheath and throwing it with deadly accuracy.

As if Cherri was shooing away a fly, she knocked the dagger out of the air with a simple flick of her wrist making the scythe knock the blade aside.

Nic wheezed and coughed, he could not take much more of this and now he was defenseless.

"Surrender," Cherri ordered, "Or I will force you to submit."

Nic fell to his knees, no longer able to stand.

"A sign of submission?" Cherri laughed. "Well, a win is a win." She raised her scythe, ready to bring it down upon Nic. "See ya on the other side, kid."

Nic looked up at her and he smirked.

Cherri swung her scythe down.

Nic closed his eyes and with his last bit of energy, he phased through the floor. He fell into the room below Trisha's, as the scythe narrowly missed him. Nic hit the floor hard, not expecting to actually make it. He rolled onto his feet and held his head. He felt so sick and dizzy; just wanting to lay still and die, he felt awful.

"Ash!" Nic cried out weakly, begging for help. Nic doubted he could do much of anything anymore.

Cherri dropped through the ceiling. "Anything you can do, I can do better." She sang, twirling her scythe like a baton. "I can do anything better than you." She finished singing and stopped her scythe. With a simple flick of the wrist, as if the scythe was weightless, she attacked Nic.

Nic stumbled to his feet and retreated, trying his best to get out of dodge.

Cherri swung her scythe and Nic watched it all like it was going by in slow motion.

It was barely going to miss Nic by a few inches, which was more than enough. Nic's eyes widened in horror as he watched the scythe randomly enlarge, becoming big enough to reach him and slice Nic across the chest.

Nic cried out in pain and held his chest, dark teal goo dripped to the floor in thick pools, flowing out from in between his fingers.

Cherri pulled her scythe back and smoothly raked a finger across the blade. She looked at the teal blood dripping off her finger. "Such a pretty color," She observed and carefully tasted the familiar's blood. Cherri's face scrunched up in disgust and she spat on the ground. "A familiar's body is a weak imitation of a human husk. Leave a soul in one too long and the body taints it."

Nic held his chest, panting and wincing from the pain as blood seeped from his wound. "H-How did you... h-hit me? I was out of range."

Cherri laughed. "Oh Nicholas, I can make my scythe change its size at will."

"And I thought you said... that the scythe can only.... hit my soul?" Nic coughed, spitting up blood.

Cherri was laughing so hard that she was practically gasping. "How stupid can you be? Nicholas, to get to your soul, I have to rip your makeshift body apart by the sutures to tear your precious soul out of you."

"That's cheating." Nic gasped in pain, holding his hand tight to the wound as blood dripped through his fingers, staining the floor teal.

Cherri shrugged laughing. "You've never been in a fight before, have you?" Cherri twirled her scythe. "There are no rules in a fight. I told you that I will win tonight. It's a promise. You might as well submit. I'm not an easy opponent." She whirled her scythe around preparing to swing it once again.

"Such a big bad opponent challenging a week-old changeling." A voice mocked the reaper.

Cherri grit her teeth annoyed. "I'm only ashamed that I didn't harvest the soul before the master butted in."

The door beside Nic was kicked open and Ash stood in the doorway, holding his deck of Spellcaster cards. Ash looked down at Nic and smiled. "I believe that I was called?"

Nic sighed, relieved to have some help.

"You look like crap," Ash smirked, glancing over at Nic while making sure to keep an eye on Cherri.

"I feel like it too." Nic admitted and coughed up some blood.

Ash laughed. "At least, you're cracking jokes, you'll live."

Cherri held her scythe up, threateningly. "Don't get comfortable, I'm not done here."

Ash drew a card off the top of his Spellcaster deck. "I know. You're a reaper, a dangerous creature. As a wizard, it's my job to protect my familiar and eliminate any possible threats. I would be failing if I couldn't save Nic from a pathetic excuse of a reaper, such as yourself."

"Pathetic?" Cherri gasped, astounded by the insult.

"Absolutely. Now that I'm here, do you even want to fight us?" Ash challenged the reaper, shielding his wounded familiar.

Cherri pursed her lips and glared at Ash. "The familiar is useless to you wizard, just a weakened soul attached to a useless body. He doesn't even have the energy to escape, I've worn him down."

Ash glanced down at Nic, he knew it was true. In his current state, Nic was useless.

"I just want to save Nicholas's soul. Why can't you see that?!" Cherri yelled mostly at Nic. "But if I have to fight, I don't mind taking you one-on-one," Cherri smirked, looking at Ash, "When I'm done, I will have two souls for harvesting at the price of one. What a great deal!" She laughed.

Ash grinned. "Perfect. I took the liberty to prepare this card deck specifically for challenging a reaper; it would be a shame if I didn't get a chance to use it."

"That's only if I give you time to draw the cards!" Cherri roared and swung her scythe.

Ash revealed the card he was already holding and turned it over to show Cherri. "Activate 'Time-out'!"

The card's magic gave off a bright light and vanished from Ash's hand. The light overtook Cherri and froze her in place, unable to move. It was as if someone hit pause on a giant high-definition television.

Ash slid his deck into his back pocket and knelt beside Nic, "How bad is it?" The wizard asked, trying to look at Nic's wound.

Nic winced, guarding his injured chest. After some coaxing from Ash, Nic finally withdrew his hand from his chest, showing the wizard the deep gash which soaked Nic's torso in teal blood. Nic coughed and some blood trickled out of the corners of his mouth.

Ash carefully wrapped his arms under Nic's and dragged the familiar across the ground, leaving a trail of teal blood, to prop him up against a wall.

Nic scrunched his face up in pain as Ash dragged him, muffling a weak groan.

The young wizard knelt down and examined Nic's wound cautiously.

Nic stared at Ash, trying to look anywhere but his chest. "I'm sorry," He whispered.

Ash smiled softly and rubbed Nic's shoulder. "Hey no problem, you're in good hands. I'm the apprentice of a witch doctor, remember? I can get you healed up real quick." Ash promised.

Nic panted and looked away from Ash examining his chest. "I thought familiar's healed quickly."

"They do, but like everyone, it takes time for their blood to clot. Once the familiar's blood clots, the body will heal itself pretty fast. But your wound is deep, it will take a few minutes in the least to heal."

Nic coughed up more blood, feeling it dribble down his chin.

Ash glanced up and wiped Nic's mouth with his sleeve. "You won't die from this. A familiar's body can be completely destroyed, though it will hurt like hell, they'll live through it. A familiar will only die if the master is killed or they are fatally hit by a familiar weapon or a death scythe. The reaper only grazed you, but it's deep. The only way for this to fully heal is for familiars to have plenty of nutrients in their body." Ash informed Nic.

"The reaper said that no matter how much I drink from you, I wouldn't be strong enough to beat her." Nic coughed, and Ash put more pressure on the open wound across Nic's chest.

Ash snorted. "That's ridiculous."

"How do you know? Besides, I don't know how to fight well and I lost my familiar weapons." Nic argued his point, wheezing, as Ash rolled up the sleeve of his dress shirt.

"I have faith in you, I've seen you train with Shima. You got this." Ash encouraged, offering his arm to Nic.

Nic wearily looked at it.

Ash glanced over at Cherri. He could feel his magic draining to keep such a powerful being trapped within his spell. "You need to hurry, I can't keep that card's magic active for too much longer."

Nic held Ash's arm and he watched a blue vein pulsate beneath the skin. Subconsciously, he licked his lips and smelled the crook of Ash's arm where the vein resided. The white of Nic's eyes became black as he bared his fangs.

Ash smelled like a four-course meal ready to be dined upon.

Nic brought Ash's arm to his mouth and paused.

Ash relaxed, preparing for Nic's sharp fangs and trying not to tense up.

Nic looked at Ash's arm, coming back from his bloodlust high. He shook his head and pushed Ash's arm away.

"Nic..." Ash gasped, startled by the familiar suddenly pushing him away.

Nic covered his face, "I don't want to become a monster."

"You won't." Ash smiled softly. "You'll become my familiar."

Nic carefully peeped around his hands, looking from the ground to Ash.

Ash offered his arm again. "You are not a monster and you never will be. You're a living being that needs food to survive. You're not hurting me and you aren't doing me any harm by feeding from me. So please, take as much as you need."

Nic took Ash's hand. The aroma of his mother's cooking filled his nostrils as he smelled the succulent flesh. It was almost intoxicating and left Nic in a temporary high. The familiar licked his lips and his eyes turned black. He bared his fangs and sank them deep into Ash's arm, piercing the vein. Nic carefully retracted his fangs from the wound and put his lips to the two bite marks as blood pooled in each puncture wound. Cautiously, Nic sipped from the bite marks.

Warm blood splashed into his mouth and Nic savored it. Never in his life had he tasted anything so good. He swallowed the mouthful of blood and felt it coat his throat to ease his thirst and fill his empty stomach to satisfy his hunger. Nic drank his fill, drinking from the vein in time with Ash's heartbeat.

Ash relaxed and leaned against the wall, letting Nic feed undisturbed. It was awkward watching his familiar drink from him, so he looked at the reaper. Ash watched Cherri temporarily frozen in time and smiled triumphantly.

The smile quickly turned into a look of shock as Cherri started to break free of the spell card confining her. "Nic, hurry," Ash urged.

Nic rushed, gulping down mouthfuls.

Ash watched in horror as Cherri broke the spell with a blinding flash of light. Ash's 'Time-Out' Spellcaster card fell to his feet, ripped in half.

Ash grabbed Nic by the collar of his shirt and ripped the familiar off him, throwing him aside.

The animalistic side of Nic growled angrily at being interrupted from feeding. The familiar glared at Cherri, eyes glowing red surrounded by a background of black. Nic's mouth was covered in Ash's blood as he flashed his fangs at the reaper, warning her to stay away from his food source as Nic returned to Ash's side to guard him.

Cherri glared. "Familiars are disgusting creatures only driven by animalistic instinct."

Ash cracked a smile, not able to help it. He held the crook of his arm which was bleeding profusely from Nic's interrupted feeding session. Ash supported himself against the wall as he tried to stand and he laughed maniacally.

Cherri's glare shifted from Nic to Ash. "What's so funny Ashton?"

"Your view on familiars." Ash answered panting, winded from laughing so hard. The effects of holding the 'Time-Out' card active for so long was hitting Ash with full force.

"What about it?" Cherri snapped.

"You hate them because they are driven purely by instinct, correct?" Ash asked.

Cherri raised an eyebrow, "Your point?"

"How is Nic feeding any different from you collecting souls?" Ash panted, holding his bloody arm.

Cherri twirled her scythe, still working out the kinks in the spell that was previously holding her hostage. "It's my job."

"But you do it all the time. It's natural instinct for a reaper to harvest a lost soul, the same way its instinct for a familiar to protect their witch or wizard."

"Is it instinct for you to be all talk and no action?" Cherri scoffed swinging her scythe threateningly as she approached Ash. "I would rather only collect souls on my roster. But you are pushing me to make an exception, Ashton."

When Cherri came too close, Nic stepped forward to hiss and growl at the reaper, fangs bared like a feral animal to protect his quarry.

Cherri glared at Nic. "I want his soul," She said, looking at Nic but speaking to Ash. "The longer you hold onto it the more corrupt it will become."

"I'm not giving you anything." Ash crossed his arms.

"Then I will take it." Cherri reached out to grab the familiar, but her hands were knocked to the side.

Nic hissed threateningly, ready to defend himself and his master at all costs.

Cherri raised her scythe. "I never said that you had to be sane for me to take your soul, I'll take it now while you're out of your mind." She avowed and swung her scythe.

Ash pushed the familiar down and they rolled out of the way.

Nic woke from his trance and looked around, finding himself under a bed. He looked up to see Ash across from him.

Ash held a finger to his lips and Nic raised an eyebrow wondering what was going on.

Cherri laughed and jumped onto the bed. "Oh, are we playing hide and seek now? Am I the seeker?" She twirled her scythe and brought it down.

The scythe phased through the bed and stopped short in front of Ash's face, it came so close to him that Ash could not only see his reflection in the blade but it came barely a millimeter from the tip of his nose.

Ash muttered a curse and shifted away from the blade.

Cherri laughed again. "Can't spell slaughter without laughter. Come out boys, I only want Nicholas's soul." Cherri swung the scythe and it landed once again in front of Ash.

Ash cursed again and shifted to a new spot right beside Nic.

"We need a plan," Nic whispered.

"We need a miracle," Ash whispered back. "Where are your familiar weapons?"

"I dropped them."

"You have got to be kidding me," Ash whispered a groan. "Where are they?"

"Upstairs," Nic whispered a reply.

"Okay, here's the plan. Get your butt upstairs and retrieve those daggers, I'll cover you." Ash strategized.

Nic nodded, ready to go.

"On three, one...two..." Ash whispered.

Nic readied himself to make a run for it.

"Three!" Ash yelled.

The two rolled out from under the bed.

Ash grabbed his Spellcaster deck from his back pocket and drew the first card. "Activate 'Screaming Shadows'!" The card bared a picture of a tornado of black clouds with wide open mouths.

The light that was originally off in the bedroom began to flicker showing shadow beasts surrounding them. The shadow beasts were growing and escaping from the confines of the shadows of inanimate objects within the room such as lamps, furniture, and picture frames. The shadow beasts screamed an ear piercing wail and launched themselves at Cherri.

"What the-! What are they?!" Cherri shrieked and fought the shadows off as Nic ran out of the room.

Nic took the stairs two at a time and phased through Trisha's bedroom door. He looked everywhere for the daggers and found one on the ground by the door. But he had no idea where the other went.

The battle downstairs was raging on as the shadows attacked Cherri. Even though the shadows were doing nothing more than screaming at her, it threw the reaper off as she tried to fend off the bombardment.

Ash was wearing thin, growing weaker by the second. This fight was drawing a lot of magic from him, much more than he was use to in any mock battle. The 'Screaming Shadows' card released, leaving Ash without protection.

Cherri was beyond angry as she stormed over to the weakened wizard.

Ash pulled a card and held it up, showing a card called 'Needle Rain'.

Cherri kicked his hands, making the wizard spill the deck of Spellcaster cards and watched them scatter across the floor. The reaper twirled her scythe around and struck Ash across the face with the butt of the staff.

"Aaah!" Ash cried out as Cherri hit him. He fell down and propped himself up on his elbows.

Just a little bit away, Ash spied a 'Time-Out' card laying face up just out of arm's reach. The wizard reached out to grab it.

The death scythe came down and pierced through the wizard's hand.

Ash screamed in pain.

"Leave the card be," Cherri ordered.

Ash struggled against the reaper's blade, trying to free his hand and accidently bloodying up his other hand as well.

Cherri smirked and kicked the cards away from Ash while she had him pinned. "I'm done playing, Nicholas's soul is mine. And now, so is yours." Cherri extracted the scythe from Ash's hand and repositioned it. Ready to bring the scythe down upon the teen wizard in one fell swoop.

Ash raised his bloody hands in a weak attempt to defend himself from the reaper's scythe.

Cherri laughed. "You won't be alone long, Nicholas will follow right behind you." She promised and swung the scythe.

Thinking that this was the end, Ash waited to meet death. He closed his eyes and thought back on everything. Ash was never the wishing type, but now as death had him on his knees, only one wish echoed through his mind and body.

"I wished Nic and I never got into those stupid fights," Ash whispered.

Ash awaited his fate, but nothing happened. He opened his eyes slowly and looked up to see Nic standing in front of him.

In the last second, Nic had dropped through Trisha's bedroom floor after finding the second blade under her dresser. Nic rushed to Ash's aid and protected his master by catching the scythe with his daggers, making an 'X' out of them.

Ash quickly recovered and backed up, still weak from the drain of his magic.

Nic struggled to hold the gigantic scythe at bay with his two tiny daggers.

Ash picked up a handful of his scattered Spellcaster cards and held up the first one in his hands. "I'm done fighting, give up." Ash glared at Cherri. "I still have magic, and Nic is armed and fully energized," He warned the reaper.

The reaper glared at Nic and Ash. She pulled back her scythe, but Nic still stood ready to catch the scythe swing again, if need be. "I think I need a different approach." She contemplated aloud. Cherri smiled maliciously and waved at the two boys. Just like at Nic's funeral, a shroud of black mist enveloped her and she disappeared before their eyes.

Nic looked at Ash. "Should we just let her go like that?"

Ash shrugged, exhausted. "Why not? If she was smart, she wouldn't bother us again!" He yelled to emphasize to the reaper if she was still there.

Nic panted. "Thank goodness." He put some pressure on the wound across his chest.

Ash smiled. "When we get home, I'll fix that up good as new." Ash wheezed for a second and chuckled. "You got your butt kicked by a girl."

"Shut up, you did too! She was tough." Nic defended himself, sheathing the daggers and putting some extra pressure on his chest wound.

"You're right." Ash chuckled and looked at his bloody hands. "Can you heal these up?"

"Yeah." Nic shrugged, seeing Ash's injuries for the first time. Nic carefully licked the palms of Ash's hands were the bleeding originated. Nic's eyes turned black and his saliva reacted immediately doing wonders in the aide of Ash's healing.

Ash could feel the skin closing up and heal instantaneously.

Nic completely healed the wounds and even cleaned up some of the partially dried blood off Ash's hand before claiming that he was done.

Ash rotated his wrists and curled his hands to make sure everything was back in working order. Satisfied with Nic's cleanup, Ash grinned. "Thanks, now come on. We have a mess to clean up, and as soon as we're done, I'll patch you up."

Chapter 21

Nic feared the mess that Ash spoke of as the two exited the bedroom and looked around.

It was as if all the party-goers had suddenly dropped dead. They were lying spread out across the floor.

When Nic ran upstairs, he had failed to notice them. But now that he was no longer caught up in the heat of the moment, Nic could finally observe his surroundings and was shocked at what he saw.

"Are they okay?" Nic asked. The concerned familiar kneeled beside a football player he knew from chemistry class and poked his chest, trying to see if he would rouse.

Ash rubbed the back of his neck. "I may have put them under a sleeping spell," Ash admitted as he stepped over a girl from his art class to walk over to Nic, who had wandered into the center of the room.

"Why did you do this?"

"I didn't want any humans to get involved or hurt," Ash explained. "I didn't hurt them, the spell is harmless and will make them think that they are still experiencing the party." Ash rubbed the back of his head as he explained to Nic.

"What do we do? Are they going to wake up like this?" Nic asked, beholding the sight of everyone passed out.

"No, that is what we don't want. The plan is that we sneak them back to their homes and tuck them in bed. The spell will alter making them think they had fun at the party and went home afterward."

"When will the spell wear off?" Nic asked, nudging a new sleeping classmate.

"Daybreak?"

Nic raised an eyebrow, "Are you asking me or telling me?"

"A little of both," Ash admitted nervously. "I've never really used this spell before."

Nic sighed. "If that's how it is, we need to begin cleaning up. There's no telling when the spell will wear off."

"Okay. I'll start driving guests home. You clean up the house and put the bodies in the vehicles with their keys so I know who to drive where." Ash said, formulating a plan.

"This will take all night," Nic muttered and picked up a classmate. He dug into their pockets to find their car keys and wallet to look up the student's address on their license.

Ash did the same, digging through a different student's pockets.

Nic worked, sorting students and paused for a brief second. He swore he heard his name called. He glanced at Ash. "What?"

"What?" Ash repeated, not knowing why Nic asked him 'what'.

"You just called me."

Ash shook his head and continued working. "I need to check your ears when we get home."

"So, you didn't call me?" Nic asked.

"Why would I call you? I would just talk to you like I'm doing now." Ash muttered and groaned as he attempted to drag a human classmate who was about twice as big as him, across the room. Ash panted and paused. "I'm going to need your super strength Nic." Ash looked up at his familiar, noticing that Nic was staring off into the distance. "Dude, you okay?"

Nic snapped out of his trance and looked at Ash. "I heard it again."

"Heard what?" Ash asked before Nic shushed him and held a finger to his lips.

"Nic." A voice called, this time, they both heard it.

The two boys, literally, dropped what they were doing; unintentionally dropping the students they were carrying.

"You heard that right?" Nic whispered.

"Sure did." Ash nodded, looking around

"Is it a student?"

"Impossible," Ash stated, "They should all be under the spell card I used. It's still active."

"Nic." The voice called again.

"That sounds like Trisha's voice." Nic recognized, after hearing his name again.

"It can't be. She was the first one I put under the spell."

"Nic!" Trisha's voice called.

Nic could not take it anymore. He ran, following the sound of the voice to the screened in porch and paused.

Laying on a bench glider was Trisha, just like the rest of the party-goers she was in the same sleeping state. Besides Trisha was Cherri, her death scythe was active and she held a second Trisha captive. The second Trisha's body emitted a soft pink glow that originated from her very being.

"Trisha!" Nic gasped.

Cherri smiled. "See, I wasn't lying. Look at how your prince charming came to save you."

A tear fell down Trisha's cheek as she stared at Nic. "Y-you're alive? She told me but... Nic." Trisha whispered in disbelief as she looked at the boy she loved.

"Hi, Trisha," Nic said softly, desperately wanting to hold the girl he loved in his arms. Nic's gaze switched from Trisha to Cherri, "How can she see me?"

"Spirits can see other spirits, so I tore hers from her body."

Nic glared at Cherri.

Ash had followed after Nic when the familiar took off after the voice and he now stood behind the familiar. Ash carefully took a step forward.

Cherri held Trisha tighter with the scythe at her throat.

"Stay right there wizard or I will reap her soul." Cherri threatened.

Ash raised his hands in a temporary surrender. "We are reasonable people. How about we negotiate?"

"I'm up for making deals. One human soul for the familiar's." Cherri smirked, "Even trade."

"As if," Ash huffed. "I know you aren't stupid. A familiar's soul is worth a hundred times that."

"Well, see it this way, Trisha Roxwell is not on my roster of souls to be collected in the near future. But I will not hesitate to harvest her soul or any other soul connected to Nicholas if you don't surrender now." Cherri smiled maliciously.

"Trisha," Nic whispered.

Trisha watched her boyfriend, terrified and with tears in her eyes.

"Do you want this on your conscious Nicholas?" Cherri asked. "The girl you love will die and it will be all your fault," Cherri stated, twisting Trisha's arm.

Trisha screamed in pain as Cherri twisted the arm till the point it hurt.

"Stop you're hurting her!" Nic snarled, flashing his sharp fangs and his eyes temporarily shifting black.

"Nic," Trisha begged. She was terrified as the scythe's tip dug into her neck and Cherri pinned the teen against her own body.

"Quiet Sweetheart, I want to hear your boyfriend's resignation of defeat." Cherri smiled.

"Stop!" Nic begged the reaper.

"Nic, I don't understand. What's going on?" Trisha asked, shaking from fear and pain.

Nic was about to say something when he was cut short by Ash laughing.

Everyone paused and watched as Ash began to laugh maniacally once again that night. Ash laughed for a good minute and abruptly stopped. He composed himself and flashed a grin at the reaper. "What a pathetic excuse of a reaper harvesting souls out of order." Ash chuckled, mocking Cherri. "I thought reapers had pride in what they do, you must be the useless lackey."

"Shut up!" Cherri hissed. "You don't know what you're talking about!"

"Oh, I think I do," Ash stated matter-of-factly. "You're afraid of getting in trouble, aren't you?"

Cherri glared at the wizard.

"In the reaper organization, you must be little Miss goodie two-shoes. Always finishing your book just in time and being an excellent little worker bee. Such a shame that one little soul came along and botched everything up, huh?" Ash smirked.

"That's not what happened!" Cherri yelled at Ash.

"Oh yes, it is. That's exactly what happened. You lost respect when you could not harvest Nic's soul, so you became desperate. Look at yourself, you are willing to perform one of the biggest sins a reaper can possibly commit just to clear your book. Harvesting a soul not on the to-die roster is bad but is Trisha's soul even yours to collect one day or are you stealing from another reaper?"

"Shut up!" Cherri kept a hold on Trisha, but withdrew her scythe from Trisha's neck to attack Ash.

Ash easily dodged the poorly aimed strike, "What a shame! You want to clear your name, now your only choice is to sully your name further."

Cherri gnashed her teeth together.

Nic looked at Trisha longingly as the wizard and the reaper bantered with each other. He wanted desperately to hold Trisha in his arms.

Over the yelling slanders, Nic whispered two little words which drew the fight to an immediate halt, "I surrender."

Ash turned to Nic, eyes wide. "What are you doing?!"

"She'll hurt Trisha." Nic rationalized.

"Yeah, she may. I know that's bad, but we can't risk this!" Ash yelled at Nic.

"I'm not risking Trisha's life!" Nic shouted at Ash.

Cherri laughed. "Can't keep control of your familiar, Ashton? Some wizard you are."

Ash and Nic glared at the reaper. "Shut up!" They yelled in unison.

Cherri was shocked by the double dosage outburst.

Trisha dug her elbow into Cherri's side and stomped on her foot as the reaper was initially shocked by Ash and Nic's response, giving Trisha enough space to wiggle free.

Trisha stumbled forward, out of Cherri's hold, and ran into Nic's outstretched arms.

Nic caught his girlfriend and held her to his chest protectively, gently kissing the top of her head as she buried her face against his chest.

"Nic, you're alive." Tears clouded her eyes as she whispered against his chest.

"Not exactly, but I'll explain later." Nic smiled softly and stroked her hair.

Tears fell down her cheeks and she hugged him tightly.

Cherri looked at the three pissed off. "Such a sweet reunion makes me sick." Cherri glared and pulled out her tiny black book from her handbag, "Time is wasting. You're not the only soul I have to collect tonight Nicholas."

"That's a shame." Nic grinned. "Because, I'm not going with you."

Ash walked between Nic and the reaper across the room. He pulled out his deck of Spellcaster cards from his back pocket and drew the first card off the top. He raised it up and called, "Activate 'Iron Maiden'." The card illustrated a medieval torture device, with blood dripping off the inside spikes.

Cherri's eyes widened. "What?! You still have magic left?!" She screamed as a metal box surrounded her. There was nowhere for the reaper to escape as the iron maiden encroached upon her to lock her inside where the sharpened spikes awaited. "How?"

"I'm Ash Starnes. I always have magic in me." Ash smirked as the box entrapped her.

Nic winced as he watched blood immediately start to spill out from the cracks. He pulled Trisha closer to him and held her so she could not see the carnage.

The blood continued to ooze out of the metal coffin as Ash watched the 'Iron Maiden', his eyes never roaming.

After a few minutes, Ash finally spoke. "I'll let you out, only if you agree to leave my familiar and everyone else in peace. The 'Iron Maiden' will stay active as long as I need it. It does not require much magic to keep it active, just like the sleeping spell." Ash warned. "I'll keep you in their forever if I have to, which would be preferable."

Through gritted teeth, Ash heard a weak 'I surrender' from within the box.

"Release 'Iron Maiden'!" Ash declared. The metal box dissolved like liquid metal and returned to his hand to form the card.

Cherri staggered and fell to the floor in a pool of her own blood, weakened. "Curse you." She hissed.

Ash touched his deck of Spellcaster cards. "I have much worse in here," He warned. "So, I wouldn't even consider retaliation."

Cherri weakly used her scythe like a walking cane and pulled herself to her feet to stand.

Nic, Trisha, and Ash watched the red-headed reaper carefully.

Cherri was covered in blood and smiled bitterly, "Fine." She panted, in a lot of pain and coughed up some blood. She clicked her tongue, annoyed and extremely pissed off. "I'll keep Nicholas's page in my book for today." She looked up and glared at the group. "But I'll be back to collect his soul eventually. Mark my words, his soul will be harvested. Until then, I'll be sharpening my scythe for you, Nicholas." She hissed, with venom coating each word.

Nic gave a slight nod. "I'll be waiting."

A black cloud of mist surrounded Cherri and swallowed her up. Within a second, the reaper disappeared into the mist.

Chapter 22

Once Ash knew for certain that Cherri was gone, he sighed and flopped into a chair. "Thank god she left. I was faking all of that, I don't have enough magic in me to make a slight breeze much less trap a reaper again." He huffed, exhausted.

Nic looked at Trisha in his arms and hugged her.

Trisha held him tighter, not wanting to let go.

Ash watched the two and pulled himself back up. He dug out a cellphone from a pocket in his cargo pants. "If you'll excuse me, I have some people I need to call about a mess that needs to be cleaned up." Ash stepped over a party-goer and walked into the kitchen, leaving the two alone.

Nic looked down at Trisha and smiled. "Hi."

Trisha smiled gazing up into Nic's red eyes. "Hi."

Nic gently pushed back a bang that had fallen into Trisha's face and hooked it behind her ear so he could look into her beautiful hazel eyes.

"I-I must be dreaming," Trisha whispered in disbelief.

"Does this feel like a dream?" Nic asked, cupping her cheek to feel her soft skin against his.

"No. It all feels real, but you're standing right in front of me and hugging me. Nic, you're supposed to be dead, so why are you here? And why do you look like so different?" She asked, tenderly touching a lock of black hair.

Nic took Trisha's hand and led her outside, opening the screen door for her. "I have a lot of explaining and not enough time to do it in."

As the two ambled along the trail to the gazebo, Trisha's eyes focused on Nic, never losing sight of him. "Nic, tell me everything. I want to know."

Nic sighed and he walked her up the steps of the gazebo. "I did die in that car crash." He began and gently took Trisha's other hand to hold both of her hands. "I remember dying, but after that I was reborn as a familiar. Familiars are servants to wizards, and I'm Ash's familiar." Nic explained, trying to get Trisha to understand what took him a whole weekend to understand.

"Ash is a wizard?"

Nic nodded. "I've been with him since I woke last Saturday after the accident. When I looked in the mirror, I looked like this." Nic touched his hair, a little embarrassed. "Apparently all familiars have black hair and red eyes, it's a uniformity thing, I guess." Nic shrugged. He carefully maneuvered Trisha's hands so they wrapped around his neck. Nic then wrapped his arms around her waist and led her into a slow dance, listening to the music still coming from within the house. Trisha could not hear it, but Nic's sense of hearing picked up the slow song and he led the dance.

Trisha smiled. "I think you look good. I miss the green eyes, but the red make you seem more... mysterious."

Nic laughed and kissed the top of her head.

Trisha's smiled faded. "I missed you."

Nic hugged Trisha, "I missed you too. It hurt me that I couldn't comfort you. I tried so hard to get you to hear me, but nothing. I comforted you and you didn't even know it was me."

Trisha looked down at the ground. "Wait, Nic?" She asked, finally making the connection. "You were the dog?"

Nic nodded, blushing. "That's my animal form."

Trisha blushed, remembering all the instances she was with Nic. "Did you see anything?"

Nic looked to the side, too embarrassed to look into her eyes. "When you were changing I always looked away, I swear."

The two were awkwardly silent, never stopping or slowing their dance.

"But I saw your sketchbook," Nic admitted, breaking the silence.

Trisha blushed and nodded, seeming to be more embarrassed about the book than changing in front of Nic.

"Trisha, you're an amazing artist."

She blushed. "Thank you."

"I mean it." Nic looked at her as they slow danced, "Your pictures were beautiful."

"Thanks, Nic," Trisha said, looking at the ground still embarrassed.

Nic tilted her chin up so he could look into her hazel eyes. "I like seeing your eyes."

Trisha blushed and looked down again.

Nic hugged her, stopping their dance. "I love you." He lovingly whispered in her ear.

Trisha's blush darkened and she felt tears sting her eyes.

Nic held her close. "I remember seeing you in the first time in first grade. The first thing I wanted to do was ask you out." Nic ran his fingers through the curls in her ponytail

Trisha was speechless, not knowing what to say.

"I wanted to be your friend so bad, that I forgot about Ash and only focused on you. We became best of friends and it scared me. I feared that if I asked you out it would ruin our friendship. I didn't want to lose you, you're my best friend."

Trisha pushed Nic away and looked up into his red eyes. She took a deep breath and looked up at him with conviction, "I'm your girlfriend." She stood on her tip toes and kissed Nic without warning.

Nic was shocked by Trisha's small outburst and the kiss, but he quickly relaxed into it. He wrapped his arms around her waist and leaned into the kiss trying to draw it out.

"Ahem." Coughed a stranger as they cleared their throat.

Nic and Trisha broke their kiss and looked up at Jacob.

Jacob watched the two lovers and smiled sadly. "Ash called Shima and me to help clean up," Jacob explained to Nic mostly. "We need to get Miss Trisha back in her body. The longer a soul remains detached, the harder it is to put it back in."

Trisha looked up at Nic, clinging to his chest.

Nic held her close and kissed the top of her head. He wrapped an arm around her shoulder and she leaned her head against him.

The three walked inside the house to hear a 'bang', followed by Shima yelling at Ash. "Dammit! Watch the corners, you're going to give your own classmates brain damage at this rate!"

Jacob chuckled and led the two to Trisha's body, which was still laying on the glider. Jacob rolled up the sleeves of his dress shirt. "I'm going to warn you Miss Roxwell when I put you back, you will have no memory of this whole ordeal occurring."

"What?" Trisha and Nic gasped in unison.

"I'll forget Nic?" Trisha asked, looking up at her boyfriend.

"This whole event was never supposed to happen. Just be thankful that you got to see Nic again in the first place." Jacob said.

"But I can't just leave Nic like this," Trisha whispered, scared.

Nic kissed her forehead. "I'm okay Trisha. I'll be fine. I'm in good hands."

"But Nic," Trisha began.

"Don't worry Trisha," Ash said, walking in as Shima followed behind. "I'll keep your boyfriend safe. I promise."

Nic rolled his eyes and winked at Trisha before kissing her hand. "I'll always be here. You just may not be able to see me all the time, but I'll still be here."

"By why do you have to be like this, why don't you want to go to heaven?" Trisha asked.

Nic kissed her forehead. "My brother once said that death is different for a young person. Someone who dies when they are older has had plenty of time to do things in this world, the worst thing they die with is regret. But when a young person dies, it's because of two things. They either gave up trying in life or they gave their best but was stopped too early. My life isn't over yet, I still have work to do. I won't give up trying in life when I still have things to strive for. I refuse to fail twice." Nic assured her, determination coating his words.

Trisha sniffed, trying to keep her tears in. "I understand."

"Hey," Nic said, tilting her chin up as she tried to look at the ground again. "I love you," He said softly.

Trisha licked her dry lips. "I love you too," She whispered, trying not to choke on her tears.

"Whenever you two are ready." Jacob interrupted after a brief silence between the two.

Trisha hugged Nic.

Nic smiled and held Trisha, knowing this was his final time. "Just remember I'll always be here for you." He gently cupped her cheek. "Trisha, may I kiss you one last time?" He whispered against her lips.

"You never had to ask me," She answered, wrapping her arms around Nic's neck.

Nic pressed his lips against Trisha's and kissed the girl he loved. The kiss was long and passionate, but it eventually had to come to an end like all good things.

Trisha looked into Nic's eyes one final time before turning to Jacob. "What do I do?" She asked the witch doctor.

Jacob laid his hands out flat. "Lay your hands on top of mine," He instructed.

Trisha obeyed and Jacob whispered some words under his breath.

Nic and Ash watched as Trisha's pink glow brightened to a pretty hot pink.

Before their eyes, Trisha suddenly vanished.

In Jacob's hands, he held a small pink ball of light which looked like Jacob was holding a miniature hot pink sun in the palms of his hands. The wizard carried the orb over to Trisha's body and held it to her mouth.

The orb altered its shape and slipped inside the orifice.

Color quickly returned to Trisha's body and with a sudden gasp, Trisha was back to breathing normally. Just like the rest of the party-goers, Trisha was under a state where it looked like she was merely sleeping.

Ash glanced over at Nic who only stood still, watching Trisha's soul return back to her body. "Are you okay?" Ash asked.

Never saying a word, Nic walked over and Jacob let him by. As gently as he could, Nic scooped Trisha up bridal style.

"Nic?"

Shima wrapped an arm around Ash's shoulder. "He just needs to be left alone. I know that you both liked her."

Ash looked at the ground after watching Nic carry Trisha out of the room. "I liked her, but Nic loved her. I just... I was always just jealous of her I guess."

"How so?"

"For her having Nic," Ash answered.

Shima smiled sadly and kissed Ash's forehead. "I can't believe I am saying this, but you're growing up." She hugged Ash gently.

Jacob clapped his hands and rolled up the sleeves of his dress shirt. "We need to break up this little moment. We need to move, we have work to do."

Shima nudged Ash forward and the three walked into the living room to continue to clean up.

#####

Nic carried Trisha up the stairs to her bedroom.

A single tear fell down Nic's cheek as he thought of every memory he had of her; days at the park, fairs, school days, TV marathon sessions, going on 'dates'. All of it came crashing down with the realization that he will never do it again with her.

Never again could he hold Trisha and have Trisha return the sentiment. Never again could he run his fingers through her wavy hair and have her lecture him about messing her hair up. Never again could he play piano for her as she sang onstage. Never again could they run through the rain because they forgot their umbrellas. Never again could he tell her that he loved her and have Trisha tell him that she loved him in return. Never again could he comfort her when she was sad and make her feel that someone was there to help her. Never again could he hold her hand or kiss her with her even knowing of his existence. Never again...

Nic carried Trisha into her bedroom and gently laid her down. He unfolded a throw blanket and draped it over her body so she would not get cold. He bent over and kissed her cheek. "I love you."

Trisha remained undisturbed by the kiss, still under the effect of the sleeping spell.

Nic watched her, sitting on the bed. He pushed a single strand of hair out of her face. "See you in class Monday." He said softly and kissed her cheek one final time before standing and walking over to the door.

Nic opened the door and watched her sleep for a few seconds before stepping out and closing it behind him.

Chapter 23

Ash carefully bandaged Nic's chest as Jacob drove the group home.

The sun was just starting to come up in the sky after successfully cleaning up all signs of what happened at the party the night before and getting everyone safely home and in bed.

Nic looked out the window, not saying anything for quite some time. He had his vest and shirt off as Ash put the finishing touches on the bandages.

Ash made sure Nic was comfortable and helped the familiar button his shirt back on after bandaging up his chest. Ash glanced out the window and watched the sun start to rise, "Everyone should be waking up about now."

Jacob nodded and looked at Shima who was reading a newspaper in the passenger seat beside him. He smiled and rested a hand on her knee.

Ash surveyed Nic as the familiar stared out the window, "You okay?"

Nic woke from his daze and looked at his master. Nic shrugged and muttered, "I'm fine. I guess." He crossed his arms and winced from the pain in his chest. He sat stone-faced, looking at the back of Jacob's seat.

Ash did not know what to say without making anything awkward. He wanted to make Nic feel better. "I'm pretty sure the worst is behind us."

"That reminds me." Shima rolled up the newspaper she was reading and unbuckled. She turned around and whacked both Ash and Nic upside the head.

"Don't you dare do something that stupid ever again!" Shima pointed to Nic. "Your punishment for bailing you out is two weeks of extra cleaning chores and fighting classes."

Nic sighed and nodded, agreeing to the wicked punishment.

Jacob looked in his rear view mirror. "You're not getting off either Ash. We'll talk later, but you will be punished as well. First of all, you must get your grades up in school, every class even physical education. And I won't hesitate to make you lick the potion room's cauldron clean if you miss another homework assignment." Jacob threatened in his calm, composed manner which only made him seem scarier.

Ash scrunched his nose. "That's downright unsanitary, Doctor."

"So we've come to a compromise?" Jacob asked.

Ash sighed in bitter defeat and grumbled unhappily as he nodded in agreement with his uncle.

Shima smiled and turned around in her seat as Jacob pulled into the driveway of the decrepit 666 Livian street manor.

The two familiars got out without opening the doors as the wizards exited the human way.

Jacob unlocked the house and yawned, wrapping an arm around Shima's shoulders. "We're going to retire to bed. The cleanup took a lot out of us."

Ash nodded as Nic stood beside him. "Same here."

Jacob yawned and waved goodnight to the two as he escorted Shima up the grand staircase to their bedroom.

Nic yawned and stretched. "I'm going to bed."

Ash grabbed Nic's arm, making the familiar stop where he was. "I got a surprise for you." Ash smiled mischievously.

Nic looked at Ash, almost too tired to care. "What?"

"I cannot just tell you. It wouldn't be a surprise then." Ash grinned.

Nic rubbed the sleep from his eyes. "How can you have so much energy for this early in the morning?"

Ash laughed. "I've had my fair share of all-nighters."

Nic rubbed the back of his head. "I'm not exactly in the mood for surprises. I'm so tired and sleep sounds amazing right now. So unless it's a new pillow, it can wait until later when I'm actually awake."

"It's not a new pillow, but you'll definitely like it more." Ash insisted.

Nic rolled his eyes. "Fine, what is it?"

The wizard led his familiar up the grand staircase and walked down the hall. Ash stopped at the second to last door on the end, Nic's room, and blocked the doorway. "Ready?" He asked the familiar.

Nic nodded, "As I'm ever going to be." He muttered, uninterested. All he wanted was sleep and some time to let his body relax and heal.

Ash opened the door and stepped aside to let Nic in.

Nic stepped into his room and his eyes widened as he looked around.

While Nic was away at Trisha's, Ash had decorated and furnished Nic's bedroom. The previously empty walls were now lined with bookshelves filled with novels, books, journals, and binders of empty sheet music and practice sheet music. In a case was Nic's violin he found in the attic, it was restrung and ready to play; someone even took the time to polish it. Beside the violin were other new instruments such as a guitar, a drum set, a keyboard, and against a different wall was new equipment that Nic quickly identified as a makeshift recording studio. On Nic's bed was a black binder that seemed out of place in the tidy room.

Nic walked over and gently picked it up. He opened the book and realized it was a scrapbook of himself as a human. "How did you get these photos?" Nic asked Ash, looking at all the photos of himself.

Ash laughed and scratched his cheek a little embarrassed, sitting on Nic's bed. "Ummm… I kind of broke into your house to steal your families' photo albums, photocopied them, and then returned the originals to your parents."

Nic laughed and a smile spread across his face as he flipped through the book. Nic looked at each page before finally turning to the final page which consisted of different newspaper clippings of the car crash which took his life. "This is amazing." Nic looked around his newly remodeled room. "Thank you so…" Nic paused noticing Ash had fallen asleep on his bed and was snoring softly. Nic closed the scrapbook and held it to his chest. With his free hand, he gently shook the wizard's shoulder. "Ash… you're in my bed."

Ash was out like a light, never reacting to Nic's shoulder shake.

Nic rolled his eyes and smiled softly. He set the binder down and grabbed a white throw blanket off his bed. Nic unfolded it and draped it over Ash as he had done for Trisha earlier that night. Nic picked the scrapbook back up and hugged it to his chest before walking to his bedroom door.

Nic looked around his room once again in amazement and smiled. "Goodnight." He whispered and turned off the lights.

Made in the USA
Lexington, KY
08 November 2016